Vanya Says, Go!

A Retelling of
Mikhail Kuzmin's
Wings

by
Wayne Goodman

First paperback printing, November 2016

Version 1.01

13 November 2016

ISBN: 978-0-9888143-4-9

Library of Congress Control Number: 2016916705

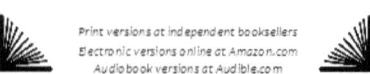

waynegoodmanbooks

waynegoodmanbooks@gmail.com
Twitter: @Wgoodmanbooks

Print versions at independent booksellers
Electronic versions online at Amazon.com
Audiobook versions at Audible.com

Vanya Says, Go!

Table of Contents

Acknowledgments

T HE FIRST PERSON I NEED TO THANK IS MIKHAIL KUZMIN for having the courage to write his original story at a time when very few people admitted their homosexual orientation in public.

However, it was actually Pytor Tchaikovsky who initially led me to *Wings* in the first place. A few years ago, I sat at my piano playing a piece by the Russian composer and thought, "What a marvelous period of time to evoke such wonderful music." I began to look into this and found that late-19th Century St. Petersburg was the epicenter of culture in Russia. At that time, there was no notion of a Gay Community, but many of Russia's best-known artists (and some members of the ruling House of Romanov) had same-sex lovers. Discovering this encouraged me begin work on another book, *Borimir: Serving the Tsars*, a fictional history that recounts the lives of two men who worked for the Royal Family during this time period.

My research led me to Mikhail Kuzmin and his writings. I found the story *Wings* a fascinating window into a bygone era and quite compelling, but it lacked somewhat in presentation. My hope is that retelling the tale will introduce a new generation of readers to this historically-significant work.

Also, I must thank the people who have read my manuscript and offered helpful suggestions: Stephen A. Smith, Daniel Brown, Carlye Knight, and my Guywriters group.

Above all, I could not have written this work without the constant support, helpful suggestions, love, and patience of my fiancé, Richard May.

Preface

I FIRST DISCOVERED MIKHAIL KUZMIN and his short novel *Wings* while researching material for another book I have written (*Borimir: Serving the Tsars*). Originally published in 1906, *Wings* was the first novel written in Russian that recounted same-sex relationships in a positive light. It tells of a young man's dealing with his realization that he is attracted to other men. Today we would call it a coming-out story.

In *Anna Karenina* (1887) by Leo Tolstoy, Count Vronsky (Anna's lover and a cavalry officer) derisively refers to a fellow officer as fat, elderly, wearing a bracelet, and having small eyes. He then refers to the officer's young page as having a feeble and delicate face. The reader is left to interpret the implied relationship between the two soldiers.

Tolstoy's sexuality is also the subject of interpretation. Although he married (the daughter of a court physician who was 16 years younger) and had 13 children (eight of whom survived), he described his attraction to the physical beauty of other men in his diary and his biography: *Childhood, Boyhood, and Youth.* Some have suggested his disparagement of the two soldiers stemmed from his own internal struggle with homosexual feelings.

During 1905, various political events throughout Russia led to more modernized and open policies. A new constitution formed the first national representative government, and many social constraints relaxed. This led to a flurry of publications from the nation's previously-oppressed minorities.

While the modern idea of same-sex culture did not exist in Russia at the time, many such couples and relationships existed. No word for "homosexuality" or "gay" existed in Russia until the 20th Century; however, such practices had existed without legal persecution for many years. Terms for the various sexual acts existed, but no general term for same-sex culture, *per se*, was used. In 1832, the government passed Article 995, a law criminalizing only the act of anal intercourse between men. It did not address sexual acts between women.

However, prosecution and punishment for its violation included loss of citizen's rights and relocation to Siberia for four to five years.

Even with these restrictions, many men and women did not hide their predilections, and several members of the governing House of Romanov took same-sex lovers openly. Some men followed the Greek model and used the term "pederasty" (from *paiderastia*, "love of boys"). This referred more to age difference and patronage, not the modern colloquial concept that involves fraternizing with underage boys.

St. Petersburg tended to be the Russian center of art, music and literature, and the city served as the hub of what same-sex social activity thrived during the 19th and early 20th Centuries, but much of that history had been subsequently expunged by the Stalin régime.

Kuzmin first read the manuscript to his circle of poet friends who then encouraged him to submit the work for publication. *Wings* received mixed reviews, and it still has its supporters and detractors today. The book appears to be the author's own coming-of-age/coming-out story as a precocious teenager.

Some of the criticism referred to a meandering plot with erratic jumps and lapses, a horde of ephemeral characters too numerous for such a short work, and that the theme of same-sex love was either too pornographic (despite no actual depictions of sexual activity) or too subtle. Many people found it radical for its time, but it opened doors for other tales of same-sex love to be published.

I have attempted to retell the tale of the orphaned boy, Vanya Smurov, from his point of view, which has allowed me to fill in some of the missing narration and address some of the other criticisms as well. The original work contained only three sections, and I choose to concoct a fourth to round out the story and provide some closure.

Mikhail Alexeyevich Kuzmin

MIKHAIL ALEXEYEVICH KUZMIN altered the year of his birth, but it is generally believed he was born in 1872 at Yaroslavl on the Volga River. His father, Alexey Alexeyevich, was already 60 when Mikhail arrived. The father almost never spoke about his upbringing, and he died when his son was barely 14 years old.

Kuzmin studied at the St. Petersburg Conservatory of Music with Nikolai Rimsky-Korsakov. A new-found love of writing verse motivated him to drop out of music school, liking poetry to manna falling "ready-made" from the sky into the mouths of Israelites in the desert.

He traveled to Egypt, Italy, and northern Russia, where he found a passion for the "Old Believers," a sect of Russian Orthodox Catholics who preferred pre-schism liturgy. Eventually, he moved back to St. Petersburg and had his first writings published in 1905. "Alexandrian Songs," a thirteen-verse cycle, appeared in the poetry journal *Vesy* the following year, and it received polite praise, but it was *Wings* that brought Kuzmin notoriety. *Nets*, his first solo collection of poetry published in 1908, brought him much acclaim.

At the time, Kuzmin lived with his clandestine lover, Sergei Sudeikin, who had married Olga Glebova the year before. When she discovered her new husband's inclinations, Glebova demanded Kuzmin move out. Despite this, the three maintained a working relationship, as well as a friendship, collaborating on plays, concerts, and poetry exhibitions.

In 1910, he met the poet Vsevolod Knyazev, and the two maintained a relationship until Knyazev committed suicide in 1913 (supposedly because a female dancer spurned him). Soon after, Kuzmin met Yury Yurkun, also a poet. They lived together with Yurkun's mother until Kuzmin died of pneumonia in 1936.

Often dubbed "The Russian Oscar Wilde," he shunned the comparison. While Wilde ended up in jail for his "love that dare not speak its name," Kuzmin lived in mild celebrity, and his works are still read today.

Kuzmin's last publication, *The Trout Breaks the Ice*, a somewhat-autobiographical narrative poetry cycle, was published in 1929. At a public reading, his followers rushed the stage and placed bouquet after bouquet at his feet.

The most recent translation of the original work, *Wings*, can be obtained from Hesperus Modern Voices (2007, ISBN 978-1843914310).

Vanya Says, Go!

Part One
Vanya says, Yes! (Да)

THIS?... THIS IS ST. PETERSBURG?

I remember thinking that the first time I rode on a train into our great city. The festive imagination of a child, thinking he'd see gleaming palaces, hordes of people milling about some great square, a military band playing inspiring marches, the train pulling through a grand entrance arch to let the passengers know they had arrived in the capital city of the most glorious country on Earth.

In reality, the tracks ran through a rather dull section of town. All I could see were old fences, cemeteries, and blocky, six-storey apartment buildings separated by ramshackle little hovels. A few early-morning milk carts rolled along otherwise empty streets. The air looked unbreathable, grey with smoke and soot.

That was in 1906, a lengthy ten years ago, and now we call our city Petrograd, a fine Russian name. When this Great War started a few years back, the government decided to leave behind the more Germanic sounding parts, 'Saint' and 'burg,' in order to distinguish us from our enemies in the Central Powers.

I have penned these words in English because Stroop, my dear Stroop, insisted he was half English, and I learned your language at his request. The editor(s) will have the burden of correcting my unintended misusage.

Mother had passed away earlier that spring, and I sat next to my cousin, Nikolai Ivanovich Smurov (who made me call him "Uncle Nika" for some silly reason) on a splintered bench in the train car we had ridden all through the night. It was early May and muggy, even at that early hour. Dawn, bright, almost-poisonous, cracked the sky. Near us sat other passengers who had boarded at some of the towns we had passed through. Many wore tattered clothes from bygone eras and their general disinterest suggested that traveling by train was an everyday occurrence for them. For me, it was only my first time in a rail car, and up until I saw those blasé people, my extraordinary experience made it seem like we were sitting on the most solid bench in the most important railcar in all of Russia.

The image of Nika's silly grin while he slept, his grey dishevelled hair and matching grey trousers with the lilac pinstripes persisted in my mind. I barely knew the man, but he had been the one to approach me after the funeral to discuss my disposition. "Your mother left no money, and you know we have very little ourselves, otherwise Natasha and I would be happy to take you in, dear cousin." He wiped at his brow the way a person who is chosen to deliver some bad news might. "As you are still studying in school, you will lodge with a family friend, Konstantin Vasilyevich Kazansky in St. Petersburg, and I shall visit you from time to time. Yes? He is a cab driver, I believe." Nika halted again, seemingly in the hope that inspiration would strike as to how to deliver additional difficult words. "It will be fun. You will meet many people who might be able to help you. Yes, the Kazansky home will be most fun indeed!" Nika then attempted a wooden smile to reassure me. "Although we have little money, I shall pay for your lodgings, and later on, if you get any inheritance at all, I shall deduct my expenses. Right?" As if a recently-orphaned teenaged boy could comprehend such business dealings. At that point, any mention of my mother brought me to the brink of tears. "And there will be other young people visiting all the time, and you will make plenty of friends, I am quite sure."

I hardly knew him, and he hardly knew me. How he could predict such upbeat things with such downright confidence amazed me. At home, I had only a few friends from school as it was. I looked at the blistered red paint on the wooden floor of the carriage thinking of the afternoon our little house filled with strange older women whom I did not remember meeting, but they all seemed to know me. They cackled and argued, fussed and fed. Their hugs and tears were meant as solace, but as these women were unfamiliar to me, it did little to stem the constant stream of tears within my own chest. My mother, the only person who seemed to care about me at all, had been taken away.

"Of course, Uncle Nika." I nodded in compliance with no idea of what I had agreed to.

The sun had just risen, and bulky shadows covered the lifeless scenery near the train. We pulled into the station and walked onto the platform, where uniformed porters scrambled to assist the wealthier-looking passengers. None of them glanced at us. Nika hired a cab on the street and we rode to the home of the Kazanskys through the dimly-lit and unfamiliar streets of St. Petersburg.

~ П ~

We pulled up to a two-storey brownstone row home in a street lined with similar houses. In my village, only the well-to-do had more than one floor, and such a place would have been considered a mansion, but here in St. Petersburg, these homes seemed rather common.

I stepped up to the front door as Uncle Nika settled with the driver. I stood staring at the polished brass knocker, and suddenly the door opened to reveal a well-dressed man staring down at me. "And whom shall I say is calling, sir?" he asked. I wanted to crawl into the shrub by the side of the stairs because he just seemed to appear out of nowhere. No one had ever addressed me as 'sir,' and his booming voice shook the very skeleton within me.

"Nikolai Ivanovich Smurov and Vanya Smurov," Nika called as he reached the bottom stair. "Konstantin Vasilyevich and Anna Nikolayevna are expecting us."

"Please follow me." The strange man opened the door fully and ushered us into the home with a white-gloved hand.

I stared at Uncle Nika wide-eyed, a question in my eyes. He caught my expression, smiled and gently shook his head side-to-side. As we walked along the main corridor, rooms opened to the left and right. A sitting room, a washroom, a parlour, all with wainscoting and striped wallpaper. Some small framed portraits hung along the way.

Voices rang from the end of the hall, "Kostya?" asked a deep, raspy woman's voice, "Are you finished with your papers? Perchance?" Followed by a man's voice, "Yes! Nothing catches my interest. If only our Russian newspapers could be as good as –"

"Nikolai Ivanovich Smurov and Vanya Smurov," announced the man as we arrived in the small, oak-panelled dining room.

The two hosts stood, approached and hugged us in turn. "Nika! How good to see you," blurted the paunchy, avuncular man. "And is this our little visitor?" He bent his head down to examine me more closely, bristly whiskers framing his pink, round face.

"Kostya!" Nika returned the hug. "Yes, this is Vanya, although he is no longer little."

"I see," said Kostya as he sized me up and down. At the time, my own whiskers had just begun to grow, and I had all the usual urges of young men 16 years of age. "No longer our Ivanushka." He laughed heartily, and the others smiled at his humour.

"Vanya, this is Konstantin Vasilyevich and Anna Nikolayevna, your new hosts," Nika introduced them, and I bowed to each in turn.

Anna approached me and clasped my hand, nearly slicing my flesh with her many, many rings. "We hope you will enjoy stay-ing with us. As you can see"–she gestured with the other hand to a nook off the side of the room where a few younger people sat eating–"you will not be the only child in our home." She nodded to them. "This is our niece, Natasha Alexeyevna. Nata? What are you up to today? Will you be occupied?"

The girl with freckles and ginger-coloured hair mumbled something unintelligible as she continued to chew on some bread with her vulgar mouth. Next to her sat another young woman and a young man. I walked to a window overlooking the back lawn and studied the plot of flagstones, grass and trees.

"That is our Koka and Boba." Each nodded to me at the sound of their names, and then returned to stirring their coffee. "Perhaps one of them can take you about and give you a tour." Anna raised her chin and eyebrows in their direction, but none of the three turned to meet her gaze. "No matter"–she walked to a table near the hallway and picked up some gloves and a hat–"Victor can get you two something to eat. I shall be attending a showing of new painters at the gallery"–she glanced at her husband who had resettled at the table with a glass of vodka–"and I expect to return –"

"Larion Dmitriyevich!" the man in the suit interrupted. He then went to the table and quickly began clearing the breakfast dishes.

Into the ever-more-crowded room stepped a real gentleman. Hat in hand, smoky-grey pin-striped suit, pointed blond goatee, sharp green-grey eyes, and a slightly receding hairline with two horseshoes of exposed scalp. How handsome and smart he looked. For the first time in my life, my manhood began to swell unbidden.

"Excuse me, please," I brushed past my new hosts, Uncle Nika, and the dashing Larion Dmitriyevich, rushed into the washroom and closed the door. The water I splashed on my face did little to quell the stirring below, and I had no idea how I was to reappear to my new hosts this way. In the mirror I caught a glimpse of my own flushed face, with its unruly dark blond hair, round grey eyes, small pouty mouth and a distasteful, flattened nose. Not very attractive at all. From a pocket I pulled my comb and began attempting to tame the rebellious curls. Once my hair began to behave, I reassessed my features and came to the realisation that everyone else in the household had thick, bushy, friendly eyebrows, but mine were thin, arched, and unfriendly.

An oval window opened to the front of the house, and I could see a group of young men in matching school jackets marching by, presumably on their way to classes. Some of them were handsome in their own right, others not so, but I watched as

5   *Part One*

the troop paraded by for my own private amusement. Perhaps they were the lads who would soon be my schoolmates.

Once everything on my own body returned to its pre-arousal status, I arrived in the dining room just as Kostya opined, "My friends, I can tell you there will be, you know, a strike! As sure as... Vanya! You have decided to favour us with your presence." He downed his glass of vodka and poured another.

As I looked about the room, there appeared to be two people fewer than when I had left. Anna Nikolayevna had spoken of going to an event, and, therefore, her absence could be accounted for. The person whom I really wanted to speak with, however, was not in sight. "Where is Larion Dmitriyevich?" I asked, my voice cracking and pathetically squeaky.

"Ah, the half-Englishman," Kostya snorted. "It is too bad for you, Vanya. He left while you were in the lavatory."

Yes, too bad, indeed.

~ Π ~

My room upstairs at the Kazanskys had a window facing the courtyard with flagstones. This view provided some comfort to me at a time I felt terribly alone in the world. The orderly, yet disordered, pattern of stones—some aligned, some misaligned—assured me the world still contained order and disorder.

One morning I rose early, as was my habit, and I stood by the window, scrutinising the variety of spaces between the flagstones, waiting for morning tea. As it was a holiday, the others slept late. I heard a distant church bell, beckoning the faithful to their sacramental duty. It made me think back on such days in my old, provincial town. My room was small but clean, with simple muslin curtains. Mother had placed her religious icons about, but not in a way that upset me. Times like these, thinking back, reminded me of how very much I missed her, and tears moistened my already-grey eyes. We would walk together to mass and stop for a meat pie on the way home. Simple, light, sweet.

St. Petersburg was not simple, light, nor sweet. The frequent rain disheartened me, organ grinders in the streets annoyed me, stacks of newspapers on the table with the morning tea, distressed me, and the chaos of these dark rooms unbalanced me.

The door opened abruptly, with no knocking, and Konstantin Vasilyevich, who insisted I call him "Uncle Kostya" even though no such familial relation existed, poked his head into the room.

"Vanya? Are you alone?"

"Yes, Uncle Kostya. Good morning. Is there something you want?"

"No. Nothing. Are you waiting for morning tea?"

"Yes. Is Auntie Anna awake yet?" Anna Nikolayevna had requested a similar epithet from me.

"Well... she is awake but not yet out of bed." He stepped in and closed the door. "I am afraid she is upset with me because we have very little money left. When she stays in bed for more than an hour after she wakes, I know that something is wrong. When we have money, she is out and cheerful. Why the change in her behaviour? Who knows? After all, just like the sun, she must come out at some point, yes?"

I knew that Kostya's brother lodged in one of the other rooms, and I only saw him around mealtime. "What about Uncle Alexei? Does he earn much?"

Kostya rolled his weary eyes. "When you say 'much,' just how much is that? My poor brother is only staying with us until his embezzlement trial is over. It seems he got caught taking a little 'much' from the till at the underground club where he worked as cashier." He looked up at a corner and resumed, "He gets a few jobs, but nothing steady. Besides, for some people"–he turned to face the direction where his wife sat awake in bed down the hall–"there is never enough money."

As I had no response, I just stared at him. He let a gloomy sigh fall and stood looking at me, as if it were my turn to say something.

After a few uncomfortable seconds, I turned my gaze back out the window. Moisture on the flagstones reflected the early sunlight with a small ripple of colours.

"The thing is, Ivanushka"–he put a hand to his mouth–"Vanya. What I meant to say is: Might you have some spare money to lend me until just this Wednesday?" My head snapped to face him. "With all certainty, I shall pay it back on Wednesday, my boy. For sure."

A fireball of disgust burst through my chest. My own family had already abandoned me to these unfamiliar people, far from home, because they felt they could no longer afford me. Uncle Nika led me to believe that the Kazanskys were well-to-do. And yet the head of their family stood before me, begging like a common panhandler.

"How did you get the idea I had any money? Where would it have come from?"

"Who knows?" he shrugged. "Unexpected things happen. You might have some coins stashed away..."

"Uncle! Please! Who would give *me* money?" His audacity appalled and offended me.

"You mean you have nothing for me, then?"

"No!"

His head dropped. "That is too bad." Kostya turned to open the door.

Even though this interview exasperated me, it had set my curiosity agog. "And just how much money did you need?"

He faced me with a toothy smile surfacing from beneath his bristly face. "Just five roubles. A little. Not much. Quite a bit. Not much at all." His eyes flashed. "So you do have some coins hidden away like a squirrel." All at once his gaze scoured the room, hoping to locate the secret spot where the money that did not exist might have been. "It would be just until midweek, you see."

"Uncle Kostya, I haven't got five roubles. I haven't even got five kopeks."

The hopeful smile become a hopeless frown. I felt even worse than before. These pitiful people were supposed to be my caretakers, not the other way round.

He sighed again. "Well, what shall we do?" Light rain began tapping on the window pane. "Still raining? Hmmmmmph." Once again, he grabbed the doorknob. "You know"–the smile returned–"Vanya... I want you to ask Larion Dmitriyevich for the money."

"Stroop?"

"Yes, yes, my dear! Ask him for me."

I cocked my head at this brash request. "And why do you not ask him yourself, Uncle Kostya?"

"I am fairly certain he would not give me any money." He lowered his eyes.

My spirit of intrigue continued. "And how is it that he wouldn't give you any money, but he would give some to me?" Honestly. Could not adults conduct their own financial business without having to enlist their wards?

"He will, believe me." The broad grin reappeared. "Please, my darling boy, just don't tell him it is for me. Tell him... tell him you need it yourself... and that you need *twenty* roubles."

"Twenty? But you asked me only for five."

"Does it really matter how much I ask? Please, Vanya, please!" His clasped hands suggested pleading or prayer.

Such a dilemma. The person responsible for my care was requesting me to beg for funds from the handsome stranger I would have liked to befriend. Perhaps this opportunity would allow me to spend some time with the mysterious Stroop and determine where his loyalties might lie.

"I guess I could, but if he asks what I want it for, what should I tell him?"

His entwined hands flew apart. "Stroop will not ask. He is too clever." I was not sure what that had to do with the question. "Besides, he likes you." My eyebrows elevated sharply. "Yes. He told me so directly."

More intrigue. "Well, just make sure you pay it back. I don't want to make a potential enemy out of a potential friend."

"Oh, certainly. Without fail." Kostya grinned, opened the door and tiptoed out.

So there you have it. My first opportunity to spend time alone with Larion Dmitriyevich. I went to the window with my back to the grey, dampened flagstones and stood there, arms crossed, considering the situation until the call for morning tea. Before leaving my room, I looked into the mirror one more time, observing the arch of my thin eyebrows and the slight gleam in my fine grey eyes.

~ Π ~

I had made two friends in Greek class, Nikolayev and Shpilevsky. They sat ahead of me but frequently turned round to pull funny faces, making the three of us burst out in laughter. The teacher, Daniel Ivanovich (a button-down, balding, grey-haired scholar in a moth-bitten wool sports jacket), gave us the stern eye but then smiled. We were his three favoured students, and we knew it, taking full advantage of the privilege.

Daniel Ivanovich would frequently disregard the homework he had assigned in favour of waxing on about the superior Ancient Greek way of life. Most of the class bored easily during these times, but Nikolayev, Shpilevsky, and I listened to these tales of heroic and historic times as if they recounted feats of modern miracles.

A breeze from the open window brushed my face and I turned to look at the treetops, pregnant with seed pods, gently swaying in unison. I missed nature and longed to remove myself from the well-ordered streets of St. Petersburg, as magnificent as they were. Having been raised in a small town, I felt the need for open spaces and fresher air. The sight of the polished brass doorknobs and cuspidors, the variety of maps on the walls, the chalkboard, the yellow box on the teacher's desk where we put our papers, the backs of the other students' heads (some with curly hair like mine, others cropped short) all taxed my forbearance.

When my attention returned to the teacher's lectern, Daniel Ivanovich stood holding a clenched fist out toward us. "The word literally translates as 'one who shows figs'," and he opened his hand to display the concealed fruit he had been holding. "Sycophants... yes, gentlemen... sycophants..."–he repeated the word using different inflections, demonstrating various nuances–"sycophants," and he folded his fingers around the plump fruit once again. "These people may have been spies or informants. When the Attic region prohibited the export of this fine fruit, sycophants (whom we might call 'blackmailers' today) would surreptitiously display a fig from under their tunic as a sort of threat to their intended target. As if to say, 'Buy my fig or I shall turn you in to the authorities'." With deft flourishes, he demonstrated such an act using the fig tucked into his hand, hiding it behind the front of his jacket, quickly giving us a peek and then returning it to obscurity. A smug smile settled upon his unshaven face.

For some reason, his expression sparked a thought: *Today I shall ask Stroop for the money Uncle Kostya requested.* I returned to gazing at the trees outside.

All of a sudden Shpilevsky bolted from his desk with a surprised look on his reddened face.

"Mr. Shpilevsky!" the teacher reprimanded, "what is the meaning of this?"

The boy turned and pointed at our other friend, "Nikolayev is molesting me, sir."

Daniel Ivanovich faced the accused, "Mr. Nikolayev, why are you molesting Mr. Shpilevsky?"

"I am not!" came the curt response.

"Well, then, Mr. Nikolayev, what exactly *were* you doing?"

"I was tickling him, sir."

The rest of us giggled.

"Silence! All of you," he roared like a hoarse mouse. "Mr. Shpilevsky, sit yourself down, and I caution you to be more careful with your choice of words in the future. As you are not a woman... unless I am completely incorrect in that assessment...," and we all chuckled, "Mr. Nikolayev is incapable of 'molesting' you. The reason being: He is only a young man with rather limited concepts." At that, we all erupted in laughter, except Nikolayev, who blushed profusely like a beet, apparently aware of the veiled insult. And to complete the manœuvre, Daniel Ivanovich flashed the fig at him while bulging his eyes. The laughter continued for a minute or so.

~ Π ~

In general, I found St. Petersburg disheartening. When I discovered the Summer Garden, at the intersection of the Neva and Fontanka Rivers, I found it demoralised me much less than other places in the city. The park spread across the landscape like a misplaced forest, and it was my favourite choice of spots to study. I tried various places throughout the vast park. After a host of locations, I decided a bench along the Swan Canal facing the Field of Mars plaza to be the least objectionable spot.

That afternoon, I brought my Teubner-edition Greek book with me, and the sun-faded, pinkish-yellow volume lay open, face-down, on my lap as I contemplated my various predicaments: abandonment into a house of disagreeable beggars; loss of my mother; distaste for the city in general; and my fascination with the very man I was supposed to request money from on behalf of my conniving uncle. People passed by, presumably absorbed in their own thoughts as I was with mine. Childish laughter wafted from the area near the tea house and Krylov monument near the Neva. A hint of river water tickled my nose.

"Busy?" came a voice from above and behind. I guess I had been so focused on my own inner workings that I failed to hear the crunching of approaching footsteps on the gravel path. I looked over my shoulder to see none other than Stroop, himself, gazing down at me with the suggestion of a smile. He bowed ever so slightly, indicated the bench with his hand and asked, "May I join you?"

His unexpected appearance startled me, and I was pretty sure he could discern my embarrassment from the unguarded look on my face. I sidled a bit to make more room. "Yes! I am busy but a bit tired of all this schoolwork. Of course, please!" I then indicated the space with my own hand to encourage his sitting next to me in this suddenly-beautiful landscape. As he sat, I started to wonder if this situation had been planned or if it were, indeed, accidental.

Stroop glanced down at my lap, "What's that? Homer?"

"Yes. The Greek class is especially awful."

"You mean you don't like Greek?" His sparkling eyes returned to mine, and an invisible shiver pulsed through me.

"Who really *likes* Greek?" I said, feeling a bit foolish about that sarcastic remark. It made me sound pretentious, but, then again, I probably was for only 16 years of age.

The corner of Stroop's mouth flinched, "That's a pity."

"What is?"

"That you don't like languages," he responded coolly, lips pouting slightly, his goatee jutting forward.

"I have nothing against modern languages–you can read just about anything–but who would want to struggle with such antediluvian nonsense in Greek?"

I could feel Stroop's eyes examining me. "What a boy you are, Vanya. The whole world–*worlds* are closed to you." He looked away and then back at me, "Though a world of beauty–not just to know, but to love. It is the basis of all education."

"But if I wanted to learn about that, I could read translated works. Why must we spend so much time learning their obsolete grammar?"

His head dropped and shook gently from side to side. I felt like I had just impaled him with a rusty pin.

"Instead of a person of flesh and blood, laughing or frowning, who can love, kiss, or hate–which one can detect in the blood surging through their veins, and the natural grace of a naked body–we are like soulless dolls, often made by artisan hands. That... that is translated. You don't need to spend a great deal of time with a preparatory lesson on grammar." He turned to face me. "The only requirement? Read, read, and read. Read–looking up every word in the dictionary–like you're wading through a thicket in the forest, and you would find untried delights. And it seems to me, Vanya, that you have the makings to become such a new, authentic person."

I just stared at this very attractive man with my jaw hanging, probably looking like an open samovar. I believed he was trying to tell me I shouldn't shirk my language studies and that if I read enough books, I could become a better person. No one had ever given me such encouragement before. If it hadn't been improper to do so, I would have leaned over and kissed him on his palpable lips.

"I can tell how you believe that bad things are all around you," he continued, "but that might actually be for the best." My eyes darted to his face. His gaze shifted toward me, and I had to look away. "Currently, you are deprived of the prejudices of a traditional life, and–should you choose–you could become a modern man."

"I don't know." He had thrown quite a bit at me. "I think I'd like to go somewhere. Get away from all this"–I waved my arm to indicate the city around us–"and Greek class... and Homer"–I touched the book cover–"and Auntie Anna. That's all."

"Into the very bosom of nature?"

"Exactly! I miss the country air, the simple food, the sweet things." I began to think about our old home and my little room far, far away.

"But, my dear friend, if you live close to nature, it means you would eat more, drink fresh milk, swim, and do little else. That would be very simple and sweet, but to enjoy nature entirely is even more difficult than your 'obsolete' Greek grammar. And, like all pleasures, it would eventually become tiresome." I hadn't considered that at all. "And I do not believe that a man who is disinterested in the city and says he prefers nature–the sky and the water–would travel to Mont Blanc to look for escape. I do not believe that he truly loves nature."

Then I remembered my mission from Uncle Kostya. "Larion Dmitriyevich, may I ask something of you?" I steeled my spine and looked him in the eye.

"Yes? What is that?" His gaze communicated a sense of acceptance and appreciation I had never received from any other person, excepting my now-dead mother. I lost my resolve and could not complete the assigned task.

"Oh, I was just wondering if you might have the time to walk me back to the Kazanskys."

He smiled and stood. "Of course, my dear friend. And along the way, you can ask me about Greek grammar."

I stood and we started walking along the gravel path together. We might have discussed Greek grammar that day, but I had no recollection of it at all.

~ П ~

A few days later, Uncle Kostya offered to take me to school in his hansom cab. Even though it was still early, the warm temperature indicated an imminent heat wave. For some mysterious reason, the street was half-blocked by *chevaux-de-frise*, those cavalry deterrents made from logs with wooden spikes through them. Kostya occupied three-quarters of the driver's seat, firmly implanted, with his legs spread wide.

As we pulled up to the school building, I said, "Uncle Kostya, can you wait a bit? I just want to see if my teacher has come yet. If he hasn't arrived, I will go with you where you need to, and from there I will walk back, rather than waiting here at the school. Yes?"

"Why would your teacher not come?" He picked up the reins and repositioned the straps in his hands.

"He's been very sick this week."

"Oh, well. Go ask, I shall wait."

I went inside to inquire about Daniel Ivanovich and found he had not shown up. Outside, Kostya sat looking forward blankly. I climbed up next to him and sat in the little bit of seat remaining.

"By the by"–he uttered before turning to look at me once more– "have you asked Stroop for the money yet?"

This whole idea seemed preposterous. The Kazanskys lived in a two-storey mansion–with a butler–in a stylish neighbour-hood. Their children attended a good school. My "Uncle" Nika paid them for my lodging, or so I believed. Anna Nikolayevna frequently attended artistic functions. Kostya earned money as a driver. How was it that he still needed me to curry favour from the man I was so attracted to?

"No, not yet, uncle."

"You know"–he said, cocking his round head forward again–"I think that Larion Dmitriyevich had some kind of premonition, brother, that we were going to ask for money. He has gone off to travel and not returned."

"Maybe he *has* returned."

"Then he would have come to call on Anna Nikolayevna, of course." He pulled the reins and the horses began their slow trot.

"Who is he, Uncle Kostya?" Perhaps I could get some inadvertent information about my mysterious new mate.

"Who? Whom do you mean?"

"Larion Dmitriyevich."

"Stroop–and nothing more. A well-to-do, half-Englishman who doesn't seem to be employed, yet he lives very well. Very well, indeed. He is well-educated and well-read. I have no idea as to why he visits us with such frequency."

"And yet he is not married, is he, Uncle?"

"Quite the contrary, even, and if our little Nata thinks she can fool him into marrying her, she is very much mistaken. I have no idea as to why he spends so much time with us. Yesterday, Anna Nikolayevna and your Uncle Alexei were shouting at each other about who-knows-what! Probably money. That's what she usually argues about…"

We crossed the bridge over the Fontanka River. Fishermen along the bank pulled the day's catches from their wire traps. Steamer boats puffed their smoke, and a crowd stood idly by one of the stone parapets. A vendor pushed a wobbly blue cart shouting, "Ice cream! Ice cream!"

"Have you heard from anyone that Stroop has returned?" Kostya looked at me with wide eyes as we pulled up to the house. "Perhaps you've seen him, yes?" The devious little smile returned to his bristly face.

"No!" popped out of my mouth before I had a chance to consider the question fully. "I mean, how could I have seen him when you, yourself, say that he is away on holiday." My face flushed.

Kostya's lowered eyebrows suggested disbelief. "You tell me the weather is not hot, but, my, how red your face has become." He hopped down from the cart, slowly climbed the front stair and disappeared into his house.

I had just lied to the man who had been giving me shelter and food, but why? What seed of mystery had sprouted around this half-English Stroop?

~ Π ~

Daniel Ivanovich, my Greek teacher, returned to school the following week. Even though he was older, perhaps my own father's age, I wanted to spend some personal time with him. For some foolish reason, I thought we could become friends. At the very least, it would give me a place to go and get away from the increasingly-annoying Kazansky home.

I waited outside the teachers' lounge after lessons, and I could hear men's voices through the thick, wooden door discussing something about Rudin, philosophy, the devil, and bones in the desert.

When the door opened, Daniel Ivanovich stepped out, still wearing the tatty tweed coat he always wore in class.

He saw me and stopped. "What do you want, Mr. Smurov?"

"I would like..." I started but lost my nerve. After a deep inhale I started again, "Daniel Ivanovich, I would like to speak with you in private."

"About what?" he tilted his balding head down toward me.

"Um, Greek, sir. I believe I need some assistance with Greek."

"But you're doing quite well in my class, aren't you, Mr. Smurov?"

"Yes, sir, I have a three plus."

"So why would you want to speak with me in private?"

My right foot began to tremble. "I, um, do wish to speak with you about Greek–in general–and... Please, Daniel Ivanovich, please allow me to visit with you at your apartment."

His tightened face relaxed into a broad smile. "Yes! Of course. Please do. I believe you have my address." He looked up at the dark ceiling and then back down at me. "This is fairly remark-able for someone doing as well in class as you are, Mr. Smurov. Yes. Please visit. I live alone and am at your service from seven to eleven."

He started toward the stairs and stopped at the edge of the carpet. "I hope you are not planning a long visit, Mr. Smurov. After eleven, I go to bed when I am at home–my own private business and I need not explain."

I stood and watched as he climbed the broad, creaky, wooden staircase. Even though his torso hid beneath the ragged, old coat, he appeared to be sinewy and vital, despite the man's advance age.

~ ∏ ~

I repeatedly sought out Stroop in the Summer Garden over the next few days after school. Even though I never encountered him, I would wait anyway, always sitting along the same path, eventually leaving without seeing him. However, I could tell my usual slow, deliberate gait had developed a certain light-ness, and I vigilantly scrutinised the men who looked a bit like Stroop as I walked along the lanes of the garden.

One day when I had finally given up yet again, I took a different path through the garden–one I had never taken before–and met up with Koka, the Kazanskys' son, who was walking along in an unbuttoned overcoat on top of his jacket. I hadn't really spent much time getting to know the others at the Kazanskys, and they hadn't spent much time getting to know me.

"There you are, Ivan. Going for a bit of a walk, are you?" He wasn't much older than me, but he was about a handbreadth taller.

"Yes, I walk here quite often. So what?" Even if he weren't slightly taller, I had gotten the sense he would talk down to me anyway.

"Why is it I haven't seen you here before?" His head swivelled to a few different angles. "Do you sit somewhere on the other side or what?" He pointed to the Swan Canal.

His inquisitiveness unnerved me and I started to walk away, "Well, anyways..."

"You know," he shouted to me, "I meet Stroop here every time, and I–uh–suspect it might be for the same reason you and I are here."

I stepped quickly back to Koka, "You mean Stroop has returned?"

He smiled down at me, "For a while. Nata and everyone knows it, and–as far as I'm concerned–I think it's beastly that he has not been to visit, as if we are some kind of stinkpot rubbish." His nose went up in imitation of a snob.

"What has Nata to do with it?"

"She fantasises that Stroop is going to propose to her, but she's just fooling herself. He's not getting married, especially to Nata"–he pointed in the general direction of the Kazansky home–"and, as far as I know, he only has æsthetic conversations with Ida Goldberg, but what should I care."

"Why should you care?" I certainly cared and was gratified that Koka shared some relevant information with me.

"I should care, but I do not," he smiled, "I am in love!" And I remember for the first time feeling jealous. Had Koka been meeting with Stroop all along, seeking his attention and affections? In my mind, Stroop belonged to me and no one else. I could only imagine that Koka had no idea of my feelings on this matter. "A wonderful girl!" He went on, much to my delight and relief, "Ida Goldberg." He smiled to himself upon saying the name again. "Educated... musical... beautiful... and how rich she is!" A smile consumed his clean-shaven face. "The only thing is... she walks with a limp." His smile diminished. "So I come by here every day. She takes her afternoon stroll between 3 and 4 o'clock, and, I'm afraid, Stroop comes here about the same time for the same reason."

If Koka was not interested in Stroop, but Stroop was interested in the same woman, it might have been problematic for me. "Is Stroop also in love with her?"

"Stroop? Well, don't you bet on it. His nose is not the end-all! The two of them just converse, but I believe she reads more into it because he is so charming. As far as Stroop's loves... well, that's a completely different area." He blew air through his closed lips dismissively.

"You're just being crazy, Koka."

"And you're being childish!" He turned his head and pointed, "Look! There they are!"

Walking through the beds of red geraniums I could see a tall girl with a pale, roundish face in a dark dress. Her very blonde hair framed a set of blue-grey eyes, like a Russian Aphrodite, and her mouth blossomed like the subject of a Botticelli portrait. She limped as she walked and leaned on the arm of an elderly woman.

On the other side of her I could see Stroop, dashing as always, his golden hair glinting in the afternoon sun. He recited, "And the people saw that all beauty, all love, came from the gods. That concept freed and emboldened them, and they grew wings!"

~ Π ~

At Nata's insistence, Koka and Boba got a box at the Imperial Mariinsky Theatre for Saint-Saëns's opera *Samson and Delilah*. The ever-scheming ginger girl with the rude mouth had selected that particular evening in hopes of meeting up with Stroop on neutral ground. However, the schedule had altered, and the performance was to be Bizet's *Carmen* instead. When Nata heard of this substitution, she fumed and raged, presuming Stroop would not attend such a well-known opera without a specific reason.

After she had calmed a bit, Nata approached me with an odd request, "If I let you attend in my place during the first act, will you leave when I arrive during the second?"

Her impertinence seemed silly to me, as were most things she said and did concerning the ever-desirable Stroop. "And what would we be attending, Nata?" Even though I knew the answer–from hearing it screamed throughout the house all the day–I decided to act innocently instead of merely playing into her devious ploy.

"*Carmen*," she snorted like one of Escamillo the Toreador's bulls. "Would you like to see it?" Her eyes bulged slightly as the gears ratcheted in her head.

I had never been to an opera before, but I knew of the great love story. "And why would I want to attend this particular piece?" I knew I was pushing a bit too far, but I seemed to be getting my own particular thrill out of taunting her. After all, we both sought the affections of the same man.

"You don't know *Carmen*?" I shook my head slightly. "Well, this Carmen girl works in a tobacco factory in Seville. Her boy-friend is the famous bullfighter Escamillo. A soldier named Don José presses his suit with her, and at the end they die together for love. Not exactly a novel by Tolstoy, but a good story nonetheless. So it is it a deal, yes?" She stared hard at me as if her intensity would convince me.

"I guess," I responded meekly, "but you're saying I'll have to leave when you arrive?"

"Yes. We only have tickets for four: Me, Auntie Anna, Boba, and Koka."

"But that way I won't be able to see the end of the opera."

"Don't worry. I've already told you, they die for love at the end."

"Oh, well. That makes it all right, then." I had to suppress a laugh of delight at watching Nata work so hard for her ambition.

That evening, Uncle Kostya conveyed us to the theatre in his cab. The four of us walked into the grand old building and I gawked at all the ornate decorations and extravagant fixtures.

Although I believed the character of Carmen was supposed to be a voluptuous temptress, that evening she was played by a thickset Russian girl. The character who really enthralled me was Micaëla, the soldier's friend from childhood who adored him, even though he showed no interest in her. Her voice and the arias she sang captured my attention, as I was also one smitten with another who did not return the desired affection.

During the second act, while people onstage danced at Lillas Pastia's Inn, Nata breezed into the box wearing a powder-blue chiffon dress. It was as if something suddenly inspired her and she sensed that Stroop had magically appeared. I knew she needed to be there, and I knew she needed me to vacate her seat.

"You have to go away now, Vanya," she whispered into my ear.

"I want to see the end of the act," I replied, although I really wanted to stay for the entire show. The music, the characters, and the situations captivated me.

"Is Stroop here?" Her neck craned about as if attempting to locate him in the darkened theatre. All of a sudden, her head stopped moving and I looked to see what had caught her attention. There, seated in a box across the circle were Stroop, the young woman from the garden, an elderly lady, and a very good-looking military officer. Nata flashed open a matching powder-blue fan to hide her remark from the others, "It was a hunch, just a hunch." She closed the fan with a snap.

Anna Nikolayevna looked over, distracted by the drama beside her. "Poor thing!" she sighed.

I stood up and allowed Nata to take her rightful place. As there was sufficient room behind the chairs, I stood and observed the rest of the act with delight.

At the second interval, I started to put on my coat, but Nata grabbed my hand, "Please, Vanya, won't you walk me to the lobby?" Her head spun back to where Stroop and his companions had risen and began to walk into the hallway. Off came the coat, which I placed over the back of a chair.

"Nata!" croaked Anna Nikolayevna, "Nata!" The echo bounced from the wall. "Would that be acceptable?"

With my hand firmly clasped by hers, Nata rushed me down the stairs. At the bottom, a large mirror filled the wall, and she stopped to re-examine and fix her unruly, coppery hair. Then, with attempted measured grace, she looped her arm through mine and guided us toward the lobby, which had just begun to fill with other audience members.

Across the room I could see Stroop standing in conversation with the handsome military officer from his box. Nata's grip on my arm increased suddenly; she must have spotted them as well. The two men must not have seen us because they walked together into the concession hall. Just on the other side of the doorway, a bored-looking woman with rather curly hair presided over a table of photographs for sale.

"Let's go out. It's terribly stuffy in here!" Nata pulled me in the direction of Stroop.

I pointed in the other direction, "But our seats are that way."

"Does it really matter?" she shouted as she pushed people out of the way with her other hand. As we reached the open door, I could see Stroop just on the other side bending over the table of photographs.

Before Nata could work her dark arts, I shouted, "Larion Dmitriyevich!"

He looked up and smiled broadly. I remember the sensation of feeling my heart melt when his eyes fell upon me. "Oh, Vanya!" Then he noticed the hideous, blue chiffon creature tightly gripping my arm. "And Natasha Alexeyevna. I am sorry, but I did not notice you right away."

She loosened her grip on my arm and batted her eyelashes with abandon. "I was not expecting to see *you* here tonight." The imploring smile seemed so silly to me.

"Why ever not? I very much enjoy *Carmen* and I'll never tire of it." He looked at his companion, then at Nata and me. "It has the deep and genuine pulse of life all bathed in glorious sunshine. I can understand how Nietzsche could have gotten so carried away by this music."

As Nata listened quietly, her malevolent, coppery eyes soaked in the view. When he finished his rhapsody, she drawled, "I am not surprised by the fact that we saw you here at *Carmen*, but, rather, that we saw you here at the theatre, instead of at our home." Another flap of her ridiculous eyelashes and she turned her head to the side, as if Stroop would take such thinly veneered bait.

"Yes, I've been back two weeks." He looked at me for some kind of assistance.

"How nice." She tugged my arm and led me along the empty corridor, past the dozing footmen, stopping at the base of the stairway to the box. I watched in amazement as her face began to fill with red splotches, and her eyes turned from copper to steel. I would have imagined she felt that Stroop–the very man she had even bothered to get dressed and show up for–had snubbed her, and spiteful anger filled her face.

The bell signalling the end of the interval rang, and I started back up the stairs to retrieve my coat so that I could leave the drama behind and go home. Nata rushed up and grabbed my arm from behind, almost pulling me down the stairs.

She had a matching frilly blue handkerchief up to her mouth. "It's a shame you had to hear that, Vanya. Shameful the way that man speaks to me," she whispered rather loudly and then ran past me, up the rest of the stairs.

After retrieving my coat from the box, and managing to avoid any further unpleasant conversation with the Kazanskys, I made my way back down to the lobby again, just in time to catch Stroop and his companion.

"Good-bye, Larion Dmitriyevich," I said and then faced up the stairs as if I were returning to our box again.

"Are you leaving?" he asked.

"Yes. I was out of place." I halted and stepped back. "Once Nata arrived, I was one person too many."

Stroop turned to his friend and then back to me, "What nonsense! Please join us in our box. We have empty seats. The last act is one of the best."

It was difficult to keep the smile constrained in my chest and not let it show on my face. The man I wanted to spend more time with had just invited me to his private box at the theatre. "No, but thanks. I'm just going to go home to bed. Besides, I'd be a stranger, not having been properly introduced to your companions."

Stroop chuckled. "That's preposterous! Come along, join us. The Goldbergs are very accommodating people, and you're a fine young man."

I followed the two men into the box. Stroop indicated a chair for me next to him, but as I started to sit, he whispered into my ear, "Vanya, you may not see me at the Kazanskys any more. However, I am always happy to see you at my home. You could tell the others I am teaching you English, but no one will ask where you are going and why. Please, Vanya, call upon me."

"Yes, of course." Was there any other answer? "Are you upset with Nata? You're not going to marry her?" I asked looking down at the dimly lit stage.

"No," Stroop responded in a serious tone.

Thank goodness. "Well, it's a good thing you're not going to marry her because she's a terrible, completely horrid, ginger frog!" I laughed, turned to Stroop, and, for some reason I might never know, grasped his arm. He didn't flinch, move or say anything about my rash act, and we sat like that through the rest of the opera. The smile in my chest slowly moved up to my warm face.

~ Π ~

The following evening, Nata ruined everyone's supper with her battle-pitched tirade about the previous night at the theatre. It was no wonder that Stroop decided to avoid any future visits at the Kazansky home. Once I had eaten a sufficient amount to discharge my hunger, and during one of the rare moments when Nata stopped to take a breath or a bite of food, I announced that I had an appointment to visit my Greek teacher for assistance with grammar. No one said anything in response, and I would have guessed that a few of them would have preferred a lesson in Ancient Greek Grammar than to have to listen to another uncouth word from Nata.

Daniel Ivanovich received me in his small, but overstuffed, apartment. Shelves full of papers reached to the ceiling. Books lay strewn about on tables and chairs. On a metal stand hung a cage with a thrush, and a paralysed kitten occupied a leather sofa. In one corner stood a bust of Antinous, the male favourite of Roman Emperor Hadrian, as if he were the house god above the hearth. This made some sense as the emperor deified the extremely handsome Antinous after he fell (or had been pushed) from a boat and drowned in the Nile River at age 19.

The teacher scurried about the room in his felted slippers while boiling water for tea and pulling paper-wrapped cheese and butter from the iron stove. All the while, the poor kitten's rheumy green eyes followed the teacher's erratic movements without making any movements of its own.

As he bustled about, Daniel Ivanovich expounded, as if lecturing an entire class. "It is interesting how we see what we want to see and understand only what we seek. As in the Greek tragedies, Romans and the Romanic people of the 17th Century saw only the three unities: action, time, and place. While in the 18th Century, it was rolling rants and ideas of liberation peppered with romance and amazing feats of heroism. Now, in *our* age, we prefer a biting tone and savagery, like Klinger's *Sturm und Drang*, which further illuminates..."

So energetic and vibrant. How did I ever get the idea he was very old when he acted so very young? Yes, he's balding, but his vitality shone through a timeworn lacquer.

"In the 15th Century," he went on, "the Italians already firmly established a view of the friendship between Achilles and Patroclus–as well as Orestes and Pylades–as Sodomitic love. However, in Homer, there is no indication of this."

Curious that he chose to lecture me on Sodomitic love. Was it that he could sense the budding feelings within me or was he, perhaps, about to make a case for his own feelings? I did have a question though, "So, the Italians made it up?"

"No, they were right, but the fact is that only a cynical attitude toward any kind of love can make it seem like debauchery. Is it moral or immoral when I sneeze or wash dust from the table"–which he had not done for quite a while, I imagined–"or stroke the kitten?" He looked around the room at the various things he mentioned. "And yet, these same actions may be criminal, if, for example–let's say–I'm sneezing to warn a killer of the time that is convenient for a murder, and so on. He dispassionately, and without malice, commits this murder, which divests this action of any ethical colouring, except for the mystical communion between killer and victim, two steadfast lovers, or mother and child."

It had gotten quite dark while Daniel Ivanovich spoke and I listened. I looked out the cobweb-filled window and could barely see the rooftops. In the distance, the darkened shadow of St. Isaac's stood out against a dirty-pink sky and clouds of smoke.

"You do such kind things, Daniel Ivanovich." I stood and started to put on my jacket. "It is getting late, and I should go home and let you commence your private time." The cat had fallen asleep on my cap, and when I tried to pull it away, the action disturbed the kitten, and it got up and limped off on his crippled front legs. "You take us into your home, we various beings in need." I scratched the top of the cat's head and shot the thrush a glance.

"I like him"—he smiled at the poor kitten—"and I am pleased to have him here with me. If you do something that gives you pleasure, and that something is being kind to others, well, that's what I am." He smiled at me. "Tell me, please, Mr. Smurov"—Daniel Ivanovich asked as he shook my hand—"was it you alone who came up with the idea of approaching me to discuss Greek?"

"Yes, but..." Should I have dared to tell him who really sent me? I had grown to like my teacher, but I preferred to keep a few things to myself. "It might have been a friend who suggested something like this."

"Ah, a friend," he nodded. "If it's not a secret, perhaps you could tell me who this friend might be." His inquisitive eyes locked onto mine and I felt compelled to respond.

"No, it's not a secret, but I don't believe you know him."

"But maybe I do. Who is he?" He certainly was persistent. Well, what harm could it do by telling him?

"*He* is one Mr. Stroop."

"Larion Dmitriyevich?" he seemed surprised but without having a surprised expression. It was as if I had mentioned the name of someone he had not heard from in a while.

"Do you know him?"

"Indeed I do. Rather well, as a matter of fact," he said as he lit the lamp at the top of the stairway for me.

As I walked back to the Kazansky house in the barest of light, I could not help but wonder how many other people knew my Stroop so well. And how many of them also fancied his attentions and affections?

Talk of taking a *dacha* to avoid the torrid, summer weather of the city had started a few days before. Some of the Kazanskys expressed the need to be back in St. Petersburg with some frequency, for either school or work, and Nata's scheme to spend time along the banks of the distant Volga seemed to sputter. The main deliberations centred around two potential locales: Terioki, which was just north of the city around the Gulf of Finland; and Sestroretsk, a little nearer, a spit of land between the Gulf and Lake Sestroretskiy Razliv.

The entire Kazansky household–including Victor, the butler–piled onto a Finnish steamer in order to get a better look at the two potential sites for the family get-away. On the trip back to St. Petersburg, Nata huddled everyone inside the boat's cabin, even though I would have preferred to hang over the rail and watch the landscape go by.

"I'm sorry, but I detest that horrible draft of wind blowing," she said to everyone and no one in particular as she entered the otherwise empty room.

"No *dachas*! No *dachas* at all," complained a weary Anna Nikolayevna once she had entered the cabin and sat on one of the rickety wooden benches. "Every place we saw was filthy, and peppered with holes–and quite drafty."

"*Dachas* are always drafty. What did you expect?" Nata retorted and then looked directly at her aunt. "This is not the first time in your life!"

Anna Nikolayevna frowned at her niece.

Koka offered his sister, Boba, a cigarette from a silver cigarette case with a naked lady carved into it. "Would you like one?" Boba turned her wrinkled-up nose away, and Koka lit up, puffing the noxious smoke throughout the small room.

"Not because a *dacha* would be the worst thing," Nata waved away a grey cloud before continuing to bore us with her rant. "They can be a bit shabby and I feel like I'm at some god-awful army camp–merely a temporary resident–and nothing has been planned. By contrast, in the city, I always know what to do and at what time."

I looked around to see if anyone else was thinking about telling Nata exactly what to do and exactly when to do it.

Anna Nikolayevna urged her on, "But what if you always lived in a *dacha*: winter and summer?"

"That wouldn't be so bad," she replied as she tousled her annoying red curls. "I'd be able to put together some kind of ordered timetable."

"That's true," her aunt responded, "You wouldn't want to settle in just for a short time and do nothing. For example, the summer before last we got so bored at this one *dacha*, we went and plastered the walls with new paper. No one would have expected us to strip off the old wallpaper. Everything was clean, and we gave the owner a gift."

"Weren't you sorry you got all sticky and pasty?" Nata pulled a disgusted face and then aimed her grimace out the window. The sun approached the horizon, and late-afternoon light reflected off the windows of the Tsar's Palace in smoothly spreading golden-pink waves that diverged all along the waterfront. "And then"–she once again broke the momentarily pleasant silence–"the masses of people, they all know about each other, what they are all cooking, what all the servants are paid..."

Anna Nikolayevna concurred. "Yes, it's generally beastly!"

"So why would you want to go?" Nata croaked.

"What do you mean '*why*'?" the older woman responded. "Where else would we go? Would you have us just stay in the city during the sweltering weeks?"

"Well, why not?" Nata had already gotten on my nerves, and the others either stared at her in amazement or looked out the windows and ignored her. "At least when the sun is too hot, you can walk on the shady side of the street."

"You know your Uncle Kostya will always come up with something." She batted at the newspaper covering the face of her husband sitting next to her. Even Anna Nikolayevna showed signs of cxaspcration with her niece.

"My dears"–Nata turned to everyone in an attempt to regain their lost attention–"let us go to the Volga! There is a small, little town–Plyos, out past Vasilsursk–where we could get a *dacha* quite inexpensively, or so I've heard. A group of my friends stayed there a while back. Levitan, the painter, lived there when he was alive."

"Well," Koka began, "if it's good enough for Levitan..."

"Stop that, Koka!" Nata roared. She seemed determined to take a *dacha* on the Volga no matter what anyone else wanted.

People went back to staring out the window or avoiding Nata's intense gaze. As the boat passed by the Alexandrovsky Garden along the Admiralty Embankment, I could see a young man about my age through a window of one of the piers. He was cleaning fish in a brightly-lit kitchen, the stove blazing behind him. I could have been that boy if the Kazanskys had not taken me in. I could have still ended up being that boy if I couldn't find a way to sustain myself after the money ran out.

"Auntie Anna," I began. Everyone else turned to look at me because I hadn't said a single word the entire day. "I think I will go visit with Larion Dmitriyevich and walk home later, if that is all right with you."

"Well," Anna Nikolayevna grunted, "go ahead, dear." She fluttered her eyelashes a few times. "So, you've got a new companion. Hallelujah!" It sounded sarcastic, but I had no idea why.

"Is he a bad man?"

"I'm not saying he's bad." She looked over at a crumpled Nata. "It's just that I don't believe he's a good companion for you."

Then I remembered what Stroop had said to tell people about our acquaintance. "He is only teaching me his English."

"Hmmmph," Anna Nikolayevna snorted. "It's all nonsense, as far as I'm concerned. I believe you'd be far better off doing your regular homework."

"I disagree, Auntie, but, all the same, you know, I am going."

"Yes, go, then," she said, but it hardly sounded sincere. "Who's holding you back?"

"Kiss your Stroop for me," Nata chimed in with a snide remark.

"Well...," I had been caught off-guard. Did everyone in the house know of my affection for Stroop, or was Nata just being catty? "I believe I will kiss Mr. Stroop, and I really don't care what any of you thinks about it." This was the first time I had ever been so forthright about my predilection.

Ever since the death of my mother, I had to accept whatever discards were thrown my way. With no money of my own, I felt it unfitting to ask for anything else. "Uncle" Kostya hounded me to beg from Stroop. The audacity of these people living such a lavish lifestyle while continuing to scrounge for kopeks amazed me.

I had put up with Nata's constant nattering about the man I favoured, the man I wanted for my own. She might have been closer in age to him, but as far as charm and education, I was far superior. Her childish teasing touched a tender spot within me, the long-smouldering fuse reached its crucial point.

"But..." Boba started to say something, but I was no longer able to hold my peace, and I detonated like a keg of black powder.

"I know *you* want to kiss him!" I pointed at Nata, "but he never would want to kiss *you* because you're nothing more than an ugly ginger frog!" She reared back in outrage. "And a complete fool!" It felt good tearing into her for once after all she has put us through with her silly aspirations for my Stroop. "Yes!" I laughed. "Yes, indeed!"

"Ivanushka, please stop!" Kostya's deep voice rang out. He didn't even look up from his newspaper.

"Well, what have you got against me? Why won't you let me go? Do you think I'm still too young?" I had had it with these obnoxious people, and it was time to hit them where they would feel it the most: in the purse. "Tomorrow, I shall write to my Uncle Nika and tell him how horribly you have all been treating me!"

Kostya put down the paper. "Ivan, please stop this nonsense!" he yelled at a slightly-higher pitch.

"This ungrateful pup of a boy! He squeals like a wounded piglet," Anna Nikolayevna barked. "How dare he behave like this!" She faced me with a furrowed scowl. "After all we've done for you." Then she turned to her husband, "I told you we should not have brought him with us."

"And Stroop will never marry *you!*" I pointed at Nata. "Never! Never!" I felt like a blazing matchstick. However, just like a parlour match, the flame quickly faded away.

Out of the calm following my storm, Nata asked quietly and coolly, "Do you think he will marry Ida Goldberg, then?" Koka's head snapped toward her at the mention of his latest love interest.

"I don't know," I responded just as quietly and coolly. "I think it is... unlikely," I said trying to be as tender as I could.

"What a bunch of gossip and chinwag!" Anna Nikolayevna continued to stir the embers of the conversation. "Do you even believe this unappreciative boy's presumptions?"

"Maybe I do," Nata muttered before turning to look silently out the window at the darkening sky.

The boat gently docked and I could see the crew working at the ropes. We started out of the enclosed cabin, one-by-one, but Boba put a hand on my shoulder to keep me close to her.

"I hope you don't think us such ghastly geese, Vanya," she cooed so that only I could hear. "They are good people, and I am sure they are happy for you to have some kind of relationship with Stroop–as well as being able to provide information about this Goldberg girl–but only if you are truly serious about Larion Dmitriyevich. Please be careful." Her beady eyes landed on me. "Don't lose your head."

"What? Do you think I am betraying myself?" Her advice surprised me. This was the first time she had actually spoken directly to me since I had moved into the Kazansky house. I could not understand why she had chosen this incident to initiate conversation with me.

"Am I, perhaps, too premature with my advisements?" She cackled as we stepped onto the pier together.

~ Π ~

I walked from the landing toward Stroop's apartment with a somewhat bouncy step. At long last, I had confronted the 'ghastly geese,' as Boba described them, and made my position known. Perhaps they would respect me more in the future, but I had my doubts about that. Given the way they usually behaved, within a few days the whole incident would have faded from their memories, which were peppered with holes like a drafty *dacha*.

Stroop's butler allowed me entry, and I could hear piano music and singing. It was a man's voice; one I had not heard before. Like a siren's call, the song drew me toward it, up the stairs and down a long, dark hallway toward the parlour. Just outside the arch, I paused and listened to words I never forgot:

> *Evening twilight over the warm sea,*
> *Beacon lights on the darkened sky,*
> *The scent of verbena at the end of the feast,*
> *Fresh morning after long vigils,*
> *A walk in the alleys of the spring garden.*
> *The shouts and laughter of a woman bathing,*
> *Sacred peacocks near the Temple of Juno,*
> *Vendors of violets, pomegranates and lemons,*
> *Cooing doves, the sun is shining*
> *When I see you, my dear city!*

A dense fog of low piano chords enveloped the lyrical phrases of the melodious singing. I waited for the piece to end before stepping into the room. Men's voices had begun in various conversations. What an amazing place! So spacious, and the greenish walls resounded with the likes of Rameau and Debussy. These friends of Stroop were so unlike anyone at the Kazansky place. An academic atmosphere, a late supper, men with wine and light conversation, a study with books to the ceiling–where you could virtually sense Marlowe and Swinburne–an alcove with a bedroom and vanity, bright green wallpaper with a garland of dark-red, dancing fauns. Off to the side, a dining room, all in red copper.

They spoke of Italy, Egypt, and India. Such rapture over the poignant beauty of all nations and all times. Trips to the islands. Some off-putting, but enthralling, dissertation. A smile on an ugly face. The smell of *peau d'Espagne* to cover the scent of decay. Thin, strong fingers with rings. Shoes with unusually thick soles.

I liked it. I liked it all, not that I understood it all, but it all unquestionably fascinated me, as if attempting to look through dark glass. The details of that evening remained fresh in my memory for a very long time.

At one point Stroop, himself, stood, raised his goblet, and delivered a rather long oration that I could only retain parts of. He said much more than this, but the following was all I could remember.

"We are Hellenes, my friends. Yes. The intolerant monotheism of the Jews is alien to us. They turned away from the Fine Arts; however, they harbour an all-out attachment to the flesh, to posterity, to the seed. Throughout the Bible, there is no indication for the belief of bliss in the afterlife, and the only reward mentioned is that if you show respect for the giver of life, you will live many years on the earth."

One fellow tapped a spoon on a glass, as if acknowledging the sentiment.

"A barren marriage is a stain and a curse, and it deprives you the right to participate in worship. They seemed to have forgotten the Jewish legend that the labour of childbearing was rendered a penalty for sin, but it was not the goal of life. And the farther you were from sin, the farther you would be from procreation and physical hard work."

Some of the men turned and looked at each other and nodded.

"With Christians, it is vaguely understood that a woman prays and cleanses after giving birth–but not after the marriage–however, a man is not required to do the same. Love has no purpose other than itself. Nature is also deprived of any ideal shadow of finality. The laws of Nature are in a completely different category from the laws of humans and their so-called God. The laws of Nature are more along the lines of: Not that this tree *should* bring forth its fruit, but that under certain conditions it *might* bear fruit, while in others it *will*, and may even die itself, simply and justly as it would have brought forth fruit."

Stroop paused to take a sip of his wine. After daubing his lips with a small silk napkin, he continued.

"With the introduction of a knife into it, a heart may stop beating. There is no finality, no good, no evil. And the laws of Nature can only be broken by the one who can kiss his own eyes without them being torn from their sockets, and the one who can see the back of his own head without a mirror. And when you hear, 'That's unnatural!' just look at the blind man who said it and pass by without transmuting into a sparrow that flies from the flower-garden scarecrow."

Someone next to me tried to catch my eye. His face displayed confusion. That made sense as I had a bit of trouble catching some the meaning as well.

"People walk about like blind men–or even dead men–when they could just as easily create an extraordinary life, where all pleasures would be so intensified. As if you had been born and then died in a single day. This deep desire is the only requirement for enjoying your life."

Yes, at times I have felt like a blind man without a direction. I had hopes that in getting to know Stroop, my eyes would be opened and my sight restored.

"There are miracles around us at every step: We have muscles and ligaments in our human body that cannot be observed unless they pulsate! And if you link the concept of beauty with that of women's beauty, you are only being vulgar and lustful, which is farther... farthest away from the ideal of true beauty. We are Hellenes, my friends. Yes. The lovers of beauty. Bacchanalia and the life to come. The visions of Tannhäuser in the grotto of Venus, the clairvoyance of Klinger and Thoma. The land of our ancestors, sunlit and free, filled with beautiful and courageous people."

He turned and faced the window, holding up the nearly-empty goblet. "*There*, across the sea, through the mist and darkness, *there* is where we go: Argonauts! And in the most unheard-of novelty, we learn of our most ancient roots and experience the most wonderful illumination of our common fatherland!"

The other gentlemen rose to their feet, raised their glasses and cheered, "To Greece!" Larion Dmitriyevich appeared to be the youngest of the lot, the rest looked to be about the age of my Greek teacher, Daniel Ivanovich, or even older.

Stroop then saw me standing in the doorway. He smiled and waved me over to where he was standing, next to a table with various carafes and glasses. As I made my way through the crowd of academicians, he took an empty glass, poured some water from a pitcher into it and filled the rest with a dark, red wine.

He handed me the glass, raised his and toasted, "To Greece!" and took a swallow. I repeated his toast and took a drink of the watered-down wine. He chuckled and put an arm around my shoulder. "Vanya! How good to see you. I am glad you are here. I want to discuss your education."

Education was probably the last thing I wished to discuss with my handsome Stroop. However, it was his home, and I wanted to be able to spend as much time with him as possible. "My education, sir?"

He laughed again. "There is no need for such formality here. We are all friends. Call me Larion Dmitriyevich, or Stroop, as you like." He patted my shoulder, and I turned my head to examine his sturdy-looking fingers. His hands looked like the type you would expect to see on a farmer or labourer, strong and muscular. However, instead of calluses, his skin appeared smooth and his fingernails manicured.

"Yes, of course. We are friends. How silly of me." His smooth, manicured hand felt reassuring on my shoulder.

"You need to learn more about Greece, and you should also study the classic texts. Who is your Greek instructor at the school?" He gazed down into my face.

I didn't respond straightaway because I made the mistake of looking back into his eyes. Seeing my own reflection startled me and compelled me to answer, "I believe you know him, Daniel Ivanovich."

"Daniel Ivanovich," he mused. "Ah, yes, scrawny fellow, balding, likes to take in wounded animals," he nodded.

"Yes, that's him." I found it interesting that he knew about the paralysed kitten.

"He is quite good, if I remember correctly, and I can always assist with grammar and the like." I just nodded. "However, I want you to start seeing a tutor for the Classics. Do you remember the young lady, Ida Goldberg, from that night at *Carmen*?" I nodded again. "Good. I will give you her address and I want you to call on her tomorrow afternoon. She is very learned in literature, and I believe she can further your education." He removed his hand from my shoulder and stepped to a small writing desk, from which he took a piece of paper and a pencil.

"I cannot afford a tutor, Larion Dmitriyevich. I have no money of my own."

He finished writing and handed me the paper. "No worries, Vanya. I shall cover the cost, if any. Yes, I imagine living with the Kazanskys proves to be quite challenging." His eyebrows elevated.

I took the paper and quickly glanced at the address. "Thank you... Stroop."

"You're welcome, Vanya." He looked at me again with those green-grey eyes. I could have died at that very moment and been very, very happy.

~ П ~

"Vanya, what time is it, please?" Ida Goldberg requested as she set some very colourful needlework on her lap. "The clock is in the hall."

We sat in a large room at her spacious home. In some ways it resembled a well-lit cabin on the deck of a ship, sparsely lined with simple furnishings. Some leather trunks, suitcases studded with copper nails, were not yet packed. On an up-ended chest sat a small pot of late-blooming hyacinths. A yellow curtain hung across an entire wall, covering all three windows at once, bathing the whole room in an irritating, buttery light. This was the third day in a row I visited her home after my regular school hours.

I had been reading Dante aloud so that Ida could hear it. At her request, I put the book aside and went into the next room. "Half past five," I announced upon seeing the small wall clock. As I returned to the sitting room, I observed Ida's face giving the appearance of deep thought. I took a guess, "Larion Dmitriyevich hasn't visited you for quite a while?" She looked

Part One

at me wide-eyed, as if she felt I had just reached into her mind. I picked up the Dante again. "Shall I continue?"

"I don't think we need to start another canto today, Vanya. So, where were we...? *'e vidi che con riso Udito havenan l'ultimo construtto; Poi a la bella donna tornai il viso,'* which translates to: 'and I listened to her concluding hypothesis with a smile; then I turned my eyes back to gaze on the beautiful lady'."

"'The beautiful lady.' Does that refer to meditation on an active life?"

"Not exactly, Vanya. I don't trust the analyses completely, except for historical observations, that is. Please understand, it is simple and beautiful. That's all. Otherwise—and quite rightly, I believe—instead of Dante, you will derive something much more mathematical in its place. However, I believe he might have been referring to Matelda, whom he used as a stand-in for a few abstract concepts. In fact, her name wasn't even mentioned until Beatrice says it in Canto 33." She folded her needlework, picked up a paper knife, and just sat, as if waiting for something, or someone, tapping it rhythmically on the yellow-lit arm of the chair.

After a few moments of uncomfortable silence, I blurted, "Larion Dmitriyevich will probably be here soon." That was whom I expected her attention had been drawn to.

"Did you see him yesterday?" she asked dispassionately.

"No, I didn't see him yesterday, or the day before. Yesterday afternoon, I heard, he went down to Tsarkoye, and in the evening he was at his club. The day before, he went somewhere on the Vyborg Side, but I don't know where," I reported with respect and pride.

Her eyes opened wider. "To see whom?"

"I don't know"—which was the truth—"somewhere on business, I suppose."

"You don't know," she sighed.

"No."

"Listen, Vanya"—she started, her eyes still focused on the paper knife—"I beg you—and not just for me alone, but for you, for

Larion Dmitrievich, for all of us–to find out what is at this address. This is very important. Very important for all three of us," and she handed me a piece of paper. The distinctive handwriting matched Stroop's from the address for Ida he had provided. It read:

"Vyborg, Simbirskaya Street 36, Apartment 104, Fyodor Vasilyevich Solovyov."

The Vyborg Side was primarily an industrial area that had just begun to become more residential over the last 25 years. Back at the Kazansky house, I looked at a map and found the apartment on Simbirskaya Street was across from the Finland Railway Station and the Mikhailovskaya Military Academy.

~ Π ~

The next day at school, Nikolayev and Shpilevsky made us all laugh with their imitations of Daniel Ivanovich, who had stepped out of the classroom for a minute. They took turns affecting statuesque poses with grotesque faces, until Shpilevsky began flashing a pantomimed fig at the other students while bugging out his eyes. When we heard the classroom door scrape open, the two boys leapt back into their seats.

Daniel Ivanovich looked about the room, all of our faces frozen in suppressed laughter. "I thought I heard raucous hilarity when you were supposed to be reading. What was so funny?" he asked suspiciously, and we all burst forth with amusement. I smiled at my favourite teacher, and he raised an eyebrow at me.

The idea of the fig and sycophants reminded me of Ida Goldberg's request to surreptitiously determine the importance of the address she had given me. I did not need much of an excuse to avoid the Kazanskys and spend more time with my Stroop. After school, I went to Stroop's apartment, figuring I would later give the excuse he was to help me with English, or Greek, or some other such nonsense.

The butler opened the door and escorted me up the carpeted stairway to the first floor. As I arrived at the landing, an older gentleman in an elaborate German costume was leaving. "Vanya! Come in, come in," Stroop invited, guiding me back to the green-papered study. "He is a most fascinating fellow, a dealer in Russian antiquities. I am looking to purchase some relics of the Old Believers."

"Old Believers?" I echoed.

"You are not familiar?" he asked, and I shook my head. "Ah, well. Sit down."

He filled a cup of tea for me from the samovar sitting on the table next to his chair. I took a taste of the steaming beverage, smoky and dark, like most Russian teas. To be honest, I had heard of the Old Believers before–and who hadn't?–I just wanted to hear what he wanted to say.

"As you may–or may not–know, back in the 17th Century, reformers attempted to modernise our Russian Orthodox Church." I remembered hearing about that in my holy lessons. "But a group of stalwarts rejected and resisted the changes, and they began their own church under the guidance of Archpriest Avvakum Petrov. It was a corner of the spirit world which was completely unfamiliar to me. For many years, these 'Old Believers,' as they liked to call themselves, were persecuted, much like Jews, Gypsies, and other religious minorities. However, just last year, our great Tsar Nikolay Alexandrovich signed an act of religious freedom, and all persecution was to have ended. Now that it is allowable to obtain these religious relics, some of us are purchasing and safeguarding them for future generations."

I hadn't realised that our government had persecuted so many people based on their religious beliefs. After all, any person with faith believed in much the same ideals. I couldn't understand why the way in which they practised their faith made such a difference.

"You know," Stroop continued, "there is someone I have met who is an authentic Old Believer, and I believe"–he stopped and chuckled at his choice of words–"you should definitely visit with him, Vanya." He emptied his cup. "This fellow is originally from the Volga, the old school. Not much older than you– 18 years old, I think–and he goes around wearing one of those bulky *poddyovka* jackets, does not drink tea, his sisters live in a cloister–some house on the Volga with a high fence and watch dogs, and they have to go to sleep at nine o'clock. How quaint! Yes, you should definitely meet him." He reached over and refilled his tea cup. "Tomorrow. Let's meet at his place. Stepan Stepanovich Zasadin is his name, and he has an interesting *Ascension* you must see. Come after school and I will introduce you. Take down the address. Do you need some paper?"

I set the teacup down and reached into a pocket. There I found the scrap Ida Goldberg had given me with the Vyborg Side address Stroop had written. From inside my coat pocket I retrieved a pencil.

"Good. Take this down because I will probably go directly there after my business meeting." Without having to look it up himself, he began, "Simbirskaya Street 36," and I looked down at the paper with the same address. I pretended to write so that I did not obscure what he had previously written. "Apartment 103, Stepan Stepanovich Zasadin." It was the next apartment and a different name. I wrote it down in a blank space, just in case.

The seed of mystery surrounding my Stroop continued to grow.

~ П ~

After school the next day, instead of returning to the home of Ida Goldberg, I walked across the Aleksandrovsky Bridge to the Vyborg Side. One block from the embankment, I turned onto Simbirskaya Street and found number 36. The buildings on this street were fairly new, as most of this area had been open fields until about 50 years before.

Number 36 was one of those ubiquitous six-storey, blocky buildings. I walked up to the first floor and found apartment 103. Before knocking on the door, I decided to listen for a moment, just in case Stroop had not yet arrived. The walls were not particularly thick, and I could hear a few indistinct male voices and a ticking wall clock in the next apartment, 104. The penetrating smell of sour cabbage wafted through the hallway.

I raised my arm to knock, but the door opened and I stepped aside. A fellow slightly older and slightly taller than me started through as he was just tying the belt of a bulky *poddyovka*.

"Are you Stepan Stepanovich Zasadin?" I asked.

He startled at hearing his name. "Yes. Who are you?"

"My name is Vanya. I am a friend of Larion Dmitriyevich. I was supposed to meet him here today."

"Oh, yes! Vanya. Stroop has mentioned you. However, he has yet to arrive. It might be forty minutes to an hour, I suspect. I was just on my way to pick up an icon I needed, but now I am not sure what to do. Would you rather wait here or take a bit of a stroll with me?"

He was not the most attractive man, but I imagine others might find something of interest about him. "I'll stay here." Given what Stroop had mentioned about his eccentricities and religious fanaticism, I thought it best not to be alone with him.

"Yes, yes. Of course." He opened the door fully and ushered me into the small apartment. Tables, chairs and window sills were piled with antique-looking, leather-bound books and sombre holy icons. A conspicuous blanket of dust covered just about everything, and the musty smell of the books competed with the stench of sour cabbage pouring through the open transom over the door. Zasadin picked one of the dusty books from a nearby pile and handed it to me. "I'll be back straight-away, but you can read from this while I'm gone, unless you're not interested, or you can look for something else." He scurried out the door, drawing the mouldy scent with him.

I opened the volume he had handed me, only to find it contained stories of old Russian priests, much like hagiography. Standing near the window, in hopes of escaping some of the overpowering smells, I thumbed through the pages and stopped on a story about an elderly hermit who lived in the desert and had a chance encounter with a woman who also lived there. The story went on about decomposed corpses and the inability to distinguish among them, how they were all equal before the eyes of Death, Love, and Beauty. It concluded that only Lust makes a man chase women, and a woman crave men.

Before I could get any farther, I heard a clear voice on the other side of the wall, "I'm leaving, Uncle Yermolai. Why are you going on so?"

A second, deeper voice followed, "How can you mess around and not expect me to get upset? You are a fool if you think you can keep getting away with it!"

"I believe Vaska has been making things up. Why do you even listen to him?" The younger voice sounded a bit shaky, as if he had been caught doing something he shouldn't.

"Why should Vaska lie?" the older voice asked. "He told me he refused to do it because he didn't want to spoil anything. Are you, or are you not, messing around at work?"

"Well, what about it? Yes, I mess around at work. And Vaska says he *doesn't*? On my honour, we all have indulged. Well... all except for Dmitri Pavlovich, the bathhouse proprietor," and he laughed as if making fun of this Dmitri fellow. He started again, but in a lower pitch and a bit hushed, "In point of fact, it was Vaska, himself, who taught me. One night, a customer–a real swell gentleman–said to Dmitri Pavlovich, 'I wish to be bathed by the fellow who just let me in,' and it was me who had let him in. Well, Dmitri Pavlovich knew this fellow was the type who was after more than just a bath–you know–messing around, I mean. Vaska had always taken this client before, but Dmitri Pavlovich told him, 'That's not possible, your grace, he is not a regular and does not understand your needs.' 'Well, the hell with you,' the gentleman says. 'Then give me both Vaska and this young man together!' Vaska must have heard the man's voice because he came running up and asked, 'How much would you be paying us, sir?' The gentleman considered this and then said, 'In addition to beer, ten roubles.' But we have an arrangement, you see, that whoever draws the door curtain for a client, that is who will perform the bathing, and the proprietor will not take less than five roubles for his share. Then Vaska says, 'No, sir, we cannot accept those terms.' The gentleman doubled his offer, and Vaska went to heat the water. I started to undress, and the gentleman asked, 'What have you got there on your cheek, Fyodor, a mole or some kind of birthmark?' He stretched out his hand, pointing, as he laughed. And I'm standing there like an idiot not knowing if I have some kind of mark or smudge on my cheek, or what. Just then, Vaska returned, somewhat grumpy, and said, 'Come this way, sir,' and we both followed Vaska."

"You must stop this, Fyodor," the older voice roared, "or else!"

Fyodor? I wondered if it were the Fyodor Vasilyevich Solovyov from Stroop's note.

"I think I can get a good-paying position from this."

"A good-paying position, you say?" The older man calmed a bit. "So who is this gentleman? Are you acquainted with him?"

"He lives in Furshtadtskaya Street. My mate Dmitri works as his under-butler and lives on the second storey. I have even seen this gentleman here, visiting Stepan Stepanovich occasionally."

"An Old Believer, is he?"

"No. Anyway, I don't even think he's even Russian. An Englishman, perhaps."

An Englishman? It sounded like he had pretty much described my Stroop, who just happened to live in Furshtadtskaya Street.

"Is he, you know, acceptable?"

"Oh, yes. They say he is a good, kind gentleman."

"Well, then, have a good time."

"Good-bye, Uncle Yermolai, and thank you for indulging me."

"Come back whenever you can, Fyodor."

"Yes, I will stop by soon."

Then I heard the light tapping of heels moving toward the hall-way followed by a door slamming. Without thinking about it, I rushed out the door and shouted after the fellow down the hall as he headed toward the stairs. When he turned to face me, I saw that he wore a peasant shirt under a jacket, and the fringe from his belt showed beneath its hem. He had short patent-leather boots and a woollen cap tilted to one side.

"Listen," I called out, "do you know when Stepan Stepanovich might be returning?"

The light from the door to Zasadin's apartment reflected off the man's darting eyes, and I could see his pale, grey flesh, like someone who had been cooped up and not gotten much sun-shine, almost like the colour of tundra soil. His dark hair had been cropped just at the level of his perfect, well-defined mouth. Despite some roughness of his face, there was a certain femininity to it. Even though I felt a bit prejudiced (and jealous, perhaps), his gentle, furtive eyes, the slight twist of his grin, something in his well-bred manner–which was evident even under the jacket–captivated and mystified me.

"Have you been waiting for him?"

"Yes, and it is nearly seven o'clock."

Fyodor took a look at his pocket watch. "Half past six, actually, and I am sorry if you heard us yelling. We did not believe there was anyone home."

We just stood in a locked stare, sizing each other up and down, as if we were two stags about to compete for the same doe.

"He will probably be here soon," Fyodor said, as if something, anything, needed to be said to break the tension.

"Yes. Thank you," I replied–again, just to say something. "Sorry to have bothered you." Although I really wasn't sorry at all. I just stood there feeling like steam whooshed out my flared nostrils.

"Excuse me," he grimaced, "but I must go now, sir."

Just as he turned, I could hear the front door to the building open followed by footsteps up the stairs. Before Fyodor could get very far, Stroop, Zasadin, and a tall man slightly older than me in a *poddyovka* appeared.

Stroop saw me and said, "Vanya, sorry to have kept you waiting."

Fyodor rushed to take Stroop's coat. We all stood looking at each other without saying a word. As if in some sort of dream state, I saw all this, feeling like I was falling into an abyss, and everything was obscured by a misty film.

My Stroop has been messing around with these boys at the bathhouse, paying them with beer and roubles. Our afternoons discussing Greek and English had seemed more like courtship than tutelage. He has let Nata and Ida Goldberg think he might–maybe, perhaps–marry them. For the first time in my young life I felt the horrific cannonball of betrayal punch through the pit of my gut. I felt the urge to run from the very spot, but realised I needed to remain.

Larion Dmitriyevich turned to the fellow in the *poddyovka* and said, "Sergei Sorokin, this is Vanya Smurov, the fellow I mentioned who is interested in learning more about the Old Believers."

This gave me the necessary excuse to turn my attention from Stroop. The anger and contempt continued to build up pressure inside me. I decided I would run off at the very first opportunity to do so.

Sergei, a very attractive and fit young man with curly brown hair, smiled at me as he began to remove his heavy coat, "Yes. Please come to visit us at our farm along the Volga. I'm sure my father won't mind. You can see how we live, and help with the work to earn your keep. If you are truly interested, that is."

I felt Stroop's hand upon my shoulder, and I flinched, knocking it away. "I'm sorry," I sputtered, "it's gotten late and I have to get back." I ran down the hall, down the stairs, back to the bridge, and just kept running and running, even though I really had no place to run to.

~ Π ~

When I arrived back at the dreaded Kazansky home, I needed to read more from Homer for Greek class the following day. Instead of staying in my room and just closing the door–what I normally did to keep the general craziness of the 'ghastly geese' out–I felt I needed to be around other people, and I took the book downstairs to the dining room. The light was still on, and I could see Kostya and Anna sitting at the table. For some odd and unknowable reason, the room smelled strongly of mothballs.

As I approached, I could hear Auntie Anna saying, "It is so offensive, you know, that a fellow would dishonour himself like that." When she saw me approach, her head spun in the opposite direction.

I sat by the window with my Homer, opened it and pretended to read. Konstantin Vasilyevich looked at me with disinterest and returned to his coffee.

"I have heard people refer to him as 'refined,' 'affected,' and 'overblown.' But if you continue to abuse your body–something considered natural–well, at some point you must tear raw meat with both hands, put the pieces in your mouth and fight to the death!"

The scenario he described reminded me slightly of the stand-off in the hallway with the pasty Fyodor fellow. However, I couldn't imagine ever putting raw meat in my mouth and duelling.

"You might end up chasing after rabbits or running away from wolves, *et cetera*." He paused for another sip of coffee. "You know, this reminds me of one of the stories from *A Thousand and One Arabian Nights*..."

At this, Auntie Anna stood and began making work for herself around the room while still ignoring my presence. It appeared she had heard her husband tell these stories over and over again. And now it was my turn...

"A girl is obsessed by the idea of fate, and she started asking why the various things had been created. 'Why did Allah make *this*? And why did Allah make *that*?' But when she asked about a particular part of the body, her mother whipped her and said, 'Now you see what it's for!' Obviously, the mother demonstrated her reasoning, but it is unlikely it exhausted the suitability of its uniqueness. And all the moral explanation of natural actions boils down to the fact that the nose is made to be painted green." He poked the air for effect. "Mankind has the ability to develop mind and body to the utmost. One should do what he can to seek self-fulfilment. Unless you wish to end up like Caliban, that is, misshapen and resentful."

I wasn't fully able to interpret his dissertation regarding Arabian myths, the Human condition, and Shakespearean characters, but I had some life experience. "Well, we students use our heads all the time."

"That's good to hear, and very nice to know, as Larion Dmitriyevich, himself, might have said." Kostya looked right at me, as if he delivered that statement as some sort of provocation.

"What does Larion Dmitriyevich have to do with this?" I roared back, a bit louder than I had intended, but he was a sore subject at that moment. Anna Nikolayevna stopped her busywork and glowered at me.

"Don't you think me capable of expounding upon his own peculiar opinions?" Kostya inquired. "Perhaps you find me unable to have such thoughts of my own." Tension in the room had thickened. Perhaps I shouldn't have attacked them so vigorously on the ferry boat. I honestly hadn't expected these people clever enough to have such thoughts and feelings.

"I'm going to check in on Nata," Anna Nikolayevna declared as she stood at the arch to the hallway.

"Is she not well? I haven't seen her for a few days." I may not have liked the ginger frog, but she was still one of the lodgers here, as well as a Kazansky.

"Go figure," Auntie Anna barked. "You have been gone for days on end." Her tone seemed to indicate her displeasure.

"Where have I gone?"

"I think you're the one who needs to ask yourself that," and she breezed out of the room and down the hall.

"Uncle Kostya"–he had picked up his coffee and raised the cup to get the dregs–"was it Larion Dmitriyevich you and Auntie Anna were discussing when I came in?" I figured it might be best to clear up this uncertainty.

"You mean Stroop? I don't rightly remember." He set the chipped cup back on the table. "Anna was telling me something…"

"It sounded to me like you were talking about him."

"Really? Why ever would your aunt and I talk about Stroop?"

"But do you believe he might harbour the beliefs that you expressed?"

"That is his sort of reasoning. As far as his actions, I have no idea. Another fellow's convictions are something dark and subtle."

While Kostya was a generally-disagreeable person, he happened to be one who knew Stroop better than most. "Do you believe that his actions are at odds with his words?" I needed to know whether I would eventually be able to regain trust in the man who held my broken heartstrings.

"I don't know." He threw his hands up and then poured the last of the coffee, which had most likely gotten cold, into his empty cup. "His affairs are his, and it's not always possible to act in accordance with one's desires." He took a taste of the cold coffee and wrinkled his lips. "For instance, long ago we had intended to take a *dacha*, and yet..."

"You know, uncle, there is this Old Believer who invited me to see how they lived along the Volga. He took an instant liking to me, and I have no idea why."

"Who is this Old Believer? Do we know him?"

"I doubt it. His name is Sergei Sorokin, and I met him through Stroop, who has been collecting relics from the Old Believers as of late."

"I see... through Stroop, you say?" He stared into the murky liquid in the cup on the table before him but did not take any to drink. "And you believe they would give you permission to invade their privacy?"

"Oh, yes, uncle! In fact, the Old Believer told me, 'Please come to visit. My father won't mind. You can see how we live, if you're interested'."

"But what of your schooling? Will you be forgoing the education you were sent to St. Petersburg to receive?"

Perhaps he did care about me after all. Or it could have been that he still saw me as a way to extract money from Stroop and "Uncle" Nika. "No, uncle. The schools will soon be closed for the summer months."

"Well, in that case, by all means, go, if that's what you want to do with your time." He looked down at the cold coffee again.

"I don't think auntie would give me any money, and, besides, I don't deserve it."

"No? Why don't you deserve it?" He sounded more sincere than I had expected. "Besides, didn't I ask you to speak to Stroop for some funds. Twenty roubles, I believe. Have you done so?"

Again, he wanted me to do his bidding and grovel at my friend's feet. I did not dare to mention that it was Stroop who paid for my lessons with Ida Goldberg. "It's all so disgusting! Everything is so disgusting!" My adolescent angst had fully blossomed.

"When did everything get so disgusting?" Kostya asked with seemingly genuine concern.

"I don't know." And I didn't. I just covered my face with my hands. "I really don't know." Tears started to seep from my eyes.

I heard the chair scrape and then footsteps walking away, out into the hall.

~ П ~

The next few days I endured my lessons with Ida Goldberg after school. While we continued to descend further into Dante's version of Hell together, I continued to travel downwardly into my own private Abyss of Treachery. Inadvertently discovering that Larion Dmitriyevich frequented the Turkish bath had overwhelmed my fragile ego.

I so wanted to ask her about the man in both our lives, to get her perspective on this multi-faceted object of desire, but as the tone of *The Inferno* got even darker, Ida's mood followed suit. Some days she just sat, saying nothing, not even stitching on her needlework.

One afternoon I called at her home only to find she had gone to visit Stroop. Some time had passed since my travel to the Vyborg Side and discovery of Stroop's secret, but the burning pain within me had not subsided. Perhaps this gave me justification to go to his apartment, presumably seeking my tutor, but actually to confront him about the situation between us. Her house was not far from Furshtadtskaya Street, and I walked there within minutes.

The butler let me in, and I walked up the stairs to the long hallway. In the distance, the door to his chamber was closed, which was very unusual. I could hear muffled voices on the other side, one soft and feminine, the other masculine and irate. I just kept my coat and cap on as I attempted to eavesdrop on their conversation.

After a minute or so, the handle turned, the door opened slightly, and I could see the sleeve of a red peasant shirt. Stroop's angry words pulsated down the hall, "I will not allow anyone else to be involved! Especially a woman. I forbid you–do you hear? I forbid you to speak of it!"

The door closed again, and the voices became fainter. I stood in anguish, examining the hall I had gotten to know so well. An electric light dangled in front a mirror above a small table. To the side, pegs for clothing. A pair of lady's gloves had been tossed on the table, but no accompanying hat or jacket hung on the pegs.

All of a sudden, the door to the chamber at the end of the hall opened with a bang! I saw Stroop's pale, angry face, but he did not turn my way. Before I could say anything, he started up the stairway to the second floor without seeing me standing there.

A second later, Fyodor–the pale, grey fellow from Simbirskaya Street on the Vyborg Side–wearing a red peasant shirt, entered the hall holding a tray with an empty decanter upon it.

He looked at me, but apparently did not remember or recognise me as the person with whom he recently had a stare-down in another hallway. "What do you want?" he challenged, and again I felt as if we were about to do battle over someone we both desired. His face glowed red, almost as red as his shirt, like someone who has been fighting or drinking, or both. He wasn't wearing a belt, but his curly hair had been combed straight, and I caught the distinctive scent of *eau de cologne* from Henri Brocard that Stroop always wore. "What do you want?" he repeated with wide eyes.

"Is Larion Dmitriyevich in, please?" I managed to squeak.

"He is not, sir." Fyodor lied, but with convincing banality.

"But how is it I just saw him go up the stairs?" I pointed to the other end of the hall.

"I'm sorry, but he's very busy right now and cannot possibly receive you or anyone else." His eyes darted about as the decanter began to tremble on the platter.

"Yes, well, I believe you should announce me immediately, young man!" Perhaps if I took a more confident posture, he might follow my direction.

"No, sir. Truly, it would be best if you returned another time. Right now it is quite impossible for him to receive you." Then he spoke in a more hushed tone, "He is not alone, you see."

"Fyodor!" Stroop bellowed and the manservant turned and moved quickly to the staircase, almost losing the decanter in the process.

I walked along the hall to the chamber, and through the door I could see the back of a woman with blonde curls sitting on a settee. Ida Goldberg, most likely. When I turned to leave, someone had come up the stairs without me hearing: a short woman in a green dress concentrated on adjusting her veil in the mirror. I slipped by her, but as I passed, I just glanced into the mirror and recognised the ginger frog, Nata. She started down the hallway as I started down the stairs to the front door.

~ П ~

A few days later the Kazanskys occupied their usual positions around the dining room at breakfast. Nata, Boba, and Koka sat in the alcove, Kostya and Anna at the table. When I walked into the room, no one paid me any attention. I just wanted a few slices of their stale, dark bread, some of their foul-smelling, oily butter, and a small cup of their nasty coffee.

Just as I reached for the butter knife, Konstantin Vasilyevich sputtered, "What's this?" He set down the newspaper that had been obscuring his unshaven face. "Listen, everyone. Listen to this."

Nata, Boba, and Koka stopped stirring their coffees, Anna Nikolayevna looked at her husband, and I dropped the knife back onto the dish with a clunk!

"Mysterious suicide," Kostya read to us, "Yesterday, in Furshtadtskaya Street, at the apartment of an English citizen, L.D. Stroop, a suicide."

My heart stopped. I had heard that stupid expression before, thinking it silly because no one's heart could stop without an impending death. However, at that moment, I fully understood the feeling and the meaning of the words. Had my Stroop taken his own life? He had sounded very upset about some situation, but I couldn't believe he would kill himself. At least not before seeing me one last time.

"Here's the account," he read, my heart beating once more, but now so loudly I could hear the pulse in my own ears. "A young life, full of hope, a vibrant young lady, Ida Goldberg."

Oh, no! My word. Not Stroop, but Ida Goldberg. I saw her sitting in the parlour that day. She and Stroop had words, but he left the room.

"The young fatality requested in her suicide note that we not blame anyone else for her death. The situation–which happened tragically and regrettably–appeared to be compelled by a presumed underlying romance. According to Mr. Stroop, the owner of the apartment, he had been dining with the deceased. During a heated discussion, Miss Goldberg scrawled something on a scrap of paper and then picked up the revolver he had been planning to take with him on his travels. Before he could do anything about it, the young lady fired the gun directly into her right temple. The solution to this mystery is complicated by the fact that a servant of Mr. Stroop, Fyodor Vasilyevich Solovyov, from Oryol province, disappeared the same day without a trace. The identity of a young lady who also was at Stroop's apartment half an hour before the fatal event, nor the extent of her influence on this tragedy, is not yet known. An investigation is proceeding."

Everyone in the room remained silent. The pungent smell of mothballs still pervaded the air, and the only sound was the tick, tick, ticking of the clock on the wall.

I turned toward my least favourite of the family. "Wasn't that you, Nata? The 'young lady' they referred to? Nata?" She wouldn't answer. "Don't you remember it?"

Yet no response from her. She just drew her fork around on an empty plate without saying a word.

Part Two

Vanya says, No! (Hem)

I COULDN'T TAKE IT WITH THE KAZANSKYS ANY LONGER. Those ghastly people gnawed the very sinew of my existence at every level, and I wanted to get away from them any way I could. There seemed to be no point in writing to my cousin, "Uncle" Nika, to tell him what atrocities I had to endure at his friends' home because I seriously doubted he would believe (or even care about) it anyway. Besides, he and his wife had no money either, and I certainly did not expect anything to come my way from the death of my mother, given the number of hands it would have to trickle through first.

I had no idea if Nata was the one who shot Ida Goldberg or whether my Classics tutor took her own life. That ghostly Fyodor disappeared soon after as well. Could he have killed the poor girl because of his own overpowering desires for Larion Dmitriyevich? What was clear, however, was that people who got close to Stroop ended up doing peculiar things and acting poorly.

The same afternoon we heard the news about Ida Goldberg's untimely death, I went back to the Vyborg Side apartment of Zasadin, Stroop's Old Believer connection. I asked how I could contact Sergei Sorokin, in hopes of taking him up on his offer to visit the settlement along the Volga. Without any money of my own, I had very few choices. It would either be going out to the riverside to explore their simple life or cleaning fish under a pier along the Neva River Embankment.

Fortunately for me, Sergei remembered his offer to take me with him out to his family's settlement, and after so many byzantine months in the City, I was ready to return to a less-complicated life.

A group of us rode in an old, wooden-wheeled, high-sided peasant cart as if we were a herd of small farm animals or bales of dried grass. The road to the Volga provided plenty of scenery, ranging from the cityscape of St. Petersburg to the vegetation and grassy hillsides along the riverbanks.

Their settlement in Vasilsursk looked like an abandoned mon-astery, a squat, mud-brick building with few windows. There were tables and benches near the main entrance and a court-yard where it appeared most of the activities occurred.

Of the six people there, I was probably the youngest. Old Sorokin, was the eldest, and his sons Sergei and Sasha were closest in age to me. Ivan Osipovich worked in the store during the day while the rest of us performed chores, washing, clean-ing, baking, farming. It was as close to country life as I would have liked.

One day, Maria Dmitriyevna, Sergei's mother, asked if I would like to join her picking fruit in the orchard. We walked to-gether, each holding a wooden basket to collect our spoils.

"Think about it, Vanya, how wonderful that here, a stranger– a whole other person–how his legs are different, the skin and eyes, and it is all mine, all of it, completely. You can watch him, kiss him, touch each spot on his body, wherever it is, and the golden hairs that grow on his arms, every wrinkle and fold of the skin, to the entire spectrum of your love. And you know everything about him, how he walks, eats, sleeps, the way his face becomes crinkled when he smiles, the way he thinks, the smell of his body. Then you stop being just yourself, and the two of you become one. Your flesh, your skin merges with his when you are together, Vanya. There is no greater happiness on Earth than love, for without it, there is no reason to go on. No reason at all!"

Here was another example of a woman losing herself com-pletely and becoming an emotional tragedy over her lover. I had now observed Nata, Ida Goldberg, and this woman temper their own existence for the purpose of joining with a man. I

Part Two

can only hope that when I fall in love with someone, as it appears I must at some point, my behaviour will be more considered and measured.

"And I say, Vanya, it is easier to love without possessing, than possessing without love. Marriage... marriage. The secret is not that the priest blesses you and the children arrive. Look at a cat, she can carry a litter four times a year. Marriage is about lighting up your soul and giving yourself to another completely, if only for a day, and if both souls glow, then it means that God has joined them. It would be a sin to love with cold-hearted calculation, but whoever gets touched by the fiery finger, whatever he may do, will remain pure before the Lord. No matter what, once you've been touched by the spirit of love, all is forgiven because you are no longer your own, in your spirit, your delight..."

As Maria Dmitriyevna walked from one apple tree to the next, her excitement intensified, and when she finished her oration, she beatifically seated herself on a bench, and I sat next to her. With the late-afternoon sun behind her, a golden aura formed about her silhouette. When I turned the other way, I could see half the Volga, an endless forest on the other side of the river, and, off to the right, a white church in a village nestled into a crook of the river.

"It is terrifying, Vanya," she went on, just when I had hoped her lecture had terminated. "When love touches you. It's joyful but still terrifying. As if you're flying and then everything is falling... or dying. As if it is happening in a dream, and at every moment, and every place, all you can see is the intense face of your beloved, whether the eyes, the hair, the attitude. And it's wonderful, truly. After all, here is a face... the nose–right in the centre–a mouth, and two eyes. What is it that has you so excited and dumbfounded? Indeed, many people see beautiful women and falling in love as a flower or a brocade, which otherwise might not be beautiful. Lest you reach the point of smothering change, but not by everyone, or yourself, while preoccupied with that face: What is it all about? And yet," she added hesitantly, "they say that women love men, and men love women. As it happens, women can also love women, as can men love other men. Yes, I have heard that. I even read about it in the lives of Saints: Eugenia, Niphont, Paphnutius

Borowski, even our own Tsar Ivan the Terrible. Yes, is it not hard to believe, unless it is impossible for God to put this spark into the heart of all Humankind? It is difficult, Vanya, to go against this attachment; perhaps it is committing a sin."

The sun had almost set behind the distant jagged pine trees visible in the curves of the dancing Volga, which glowed rose gold. Maria Dmitriyevna appeared to be staring at the dark woods on the other side and the pale purple evening sky beyond. I remained silent, as if I were still listening to this woman, her very essence, her mouth half open. Then all of a sudden, not sorrowfully, not disapprovingly, I asked, "But don't people sin despite everything? Out of curiosity, or pride, or self-interest?"

"It happens," she muttered, suddenly deflated. "People sin. Somehow," confessed Maria Dmitriyevna humbly without moving or turning. "However, it is difficult... so difficult, Vanya! I'm trying not to grumble, but others seem to have an easier life, and that's all right for them. To me it is like soup without salt–nourishing, but not very tasty."

I decided to just let my friends' mother go on and on along some kind of tortuous, wordy path. Even if I got very little from this experience, it seemed to give her some comfort to speak freely. Perhaps her husband did not allow for such soliloquy at home. The Sorokins generously provided me with a place to live and food to eat. It would have to get much worse before the situation even came close to the one I left behind in St. Petersburg.

She spoke of love–I think–but did she also talk about lovers of the same sex? With all her roundabout prattle, it was difficult to make sense of much of her soliloquy. People seem to think me some kind of sounding board they can bounce their long-winded orations off of. Stroop, with his meandering reminiscences of historical male companions, Daniel Ivanovich, with his talk of Sodomitic love, and now Maria Dmitriyevna, going on about similar subjects without making it clear whether she meant her or me. Perhaps because I had learned to keep my mouth shut at an early age, people thought they could just keep talking.

We walked among the trees for a few minutes more, before the sun's disk completely sank below the treeline in the west, and we walked back to the compound with only the sounds of apples ratting in our baskets and our shoes stirring up the gravel path.

~ Π ~

As the days got progressively hotter and more oppressive, meals kept moving to cooler and cooler locations. At first, we ate in the banquet hall, but when that got too muggy, we moved to a terrace overlooking the river. Soon that became unbearable and we started eating in the entrance hall because the light cross breeze kept us comfortable. When the breeze disappeared, we moved out under the shade of the orchard for a few days, and then down into the cellar beneath the monastery, a dark, vaulted, and somewhat dusty enclosure. Unfortunately, it smelled of sprouted malt, cabbage, and somewhat like mice; however, it was much cooler, and there were no flies. We pushed the large, heavy table across the room to the opposite side of the door so that we could have more light. Malanya, our cook, had to prepare the food upstairs and then run across the courtyard with it on a tray. When she stood at the top of the stairs before descending, her body blocked the sunlight and it grew temporarily dark.

"Excuse me, Lord"–she grumbled as she tentatively lowered herself down each cracked brick step–"Isn't it dark enough already? Tell me, what have you concocted whither I climb down into?" Because she had been keeping her eyes on the dark stairs beneath her feet, she bumped into Sergei, who stood holding a dish over his head, when she reached the bottom. "Well! As if I couldn't serve you myself. Why do you shadow me like that?" she asked. "I would prefer it if you –"

"You would prefer it, but now we already have it," Sergei retorted with a grin. He glided across the brick floor, slamming the dish down onto the table, right in front of Maria Dmitriyevna, which caused the metal utensils to rattle. Then he sat down between Ivan Osipovich and Sasha. "And what in God's name do you make of this dreadful heat spell?" he asked, making it sound more like a survey than a rhetorical question. "You don't need to tell me"–he went on to answer his own inquiry–"The water dries up, the trees catch fire, hard work for everyone…"

"It's for the grain, you know," Old Sorokin said while reaching for a piece of black bread.

"Yes, for the grain, for now, but if we don't do anything about it, we won't have a very big return. Nevertheless, we get water in time or no water at all. It's what God sees fit to send us." Sergei seemed to blame quite a bit on his God.

"It's not about timing. Obviously, it's penance for our sins," Old Sorokin admonished.

"But"–Ivan Osipovich intervened between bites–"there was an old-timer who died from the heat. He wasn't bothering anyone, but yet this pilgrim just withered away and died. How should we interpret this?" He was the store supervisor and the younger men worked with him from time to time, and they heeded him appropriately.

However, Sergei quietly grinned in triumph. He smiled at me and I smiled back. I found their talk about retribution confusing.

"For someone else's sins, you know, not for his own suffering," Old Sorokin decided in a tone that was not very confident.

"How so? Other people go out and get drunk," Ivan Osipovich challenged, "but the Lord goes and kills an innocent old man instead of those who have become inebriated?"

"Or else," Sergei piped in, "forgive me, let's say my father did not pay back a debt, for example, and they put me into a pit instead. Would that be right?"

"You better eat your soup instead of furthering this silly twaddle. Who? Why? What?" Maria Dmitriyevna mocked her son. "So what? Perhaps you're thinking about this hot weather. What good is that going to do? Perhaps it is thinking about you, Sergei. It means nothing."

Once everyone had finished eating, the slow and meticulous process of tea drinking started. For dessert, some ate apples, some ate preserves. I chose the apples that I had picked from the orchard with Maria Dmitriyevna.

Sergei began to reason again, "Very often it can be difficult to understand what should be understood. For example, a soldier kills a man, and I kill a man. He is called a hero and given a medal, but I get life in prison with hard labour. Why is that?"

"How can I expect you to understand?" his father questioned. "So I say, a husband and wife sleep together, but then an unmarried man sleeps with the wife. Some might look at it as if it is the same thing, but there is a difference between the two acts, wouldn't you say?"

"I don't know," Sergei responded with wide eyes.

"In the first example, the husband and wife sleeping together is one thing. They live quietly, peacefully, and they're accustomed to each other. The husband loves his wife in the same way he loves porridge or scolding a shop clerk," he glanced over at Ivan Osipovich, who just kept slurping small amounts of preserves with a spoon. "And all those follies in his mind, but in the other case it's just hee-hee, ha-ha, nothing permanent, nothing serious. Therefore, in one instance, it's the law; in the other, it's just fornication." His wife shot him a glare. "The sin is not the act, or what led up to it, it is the purpose that makes the difference."

"Excuse me," Sergei started again, "if it happens that a husband and wife love each other fully, with all their heart, and the bachelor loves his mistress just the same, whether it is while he kisses her or squashes a mosquito: how do you analyse that? Where is the law, and where is the fornication?"

"Without love"–Maria Dmitriyevna interjected abruptly–"it is something else, just disgusting."

"You say 'disgusting,' but it is necessary to know a few words in order to understand their power," her husband lectured. "That said, 'disgusting' refers to eating animals intended for pagan idol sacrifice, hares and such. That is 'disgusting,' not fornication."

"Why are you all 'fornication' this and 'fornication' that? What kind of a conversation is this to begin in front of the boys?" She raised her arms and her voice.

"Well, so what?" roared Old Sorokin in response. "I believe they can understand all of this themselves." Then he looked directly at me with one raised, bushy, grey eyebrow, "Isn't that so, young Vanya?"

I hadn't expected anyone to ask my opinion. Once again I felt like I was drowning in a choppy lake of polemic discourse. At Stroop's it was Beauty, at Daniel Ivanovich's the topic was Sodomitic Love, at the Kazansky home Kostya went on about the inevitable workers' strike, and here the theme centred around Sin. I might have been listening, but I hadn't attempted to make any sense of it. "What do you mean?"

"What is your opinion, young master," Old Sorokin prompted, "What do you believe?"

"Well, you know," I tried to stall until some idea charitably landed in my head. Then I remembered something Kostya might have said, "It is difficult to judge the affairs of others."

"You certainly speak the truth, there, young Vanya," smiled Maria Dmitriyevna. "Never judge. That's what is written: 'Judge not, that ye be not judged'."

"However, there are those who do not judge," said Old Sorokin as he began to stand from the table. "And yet, they are not free from the judgments of others."

~ П ~

The next week, Old Sorokin announced he was going to visit some people at another settlement farther up the river. We all piled into the wagon with Sergei holding the reins.

As the rickety old cart pulled up to the boat dock, various vendors had their wares on display: white bread, Caspian Roach fish, raspberries, and salty pickles. Dock workers in their colourful shirts leaned against the wooden rails and took turns spitting into the water. Maria Dmitriyevna walked her husband down the ramp to the waiting steamboat, while Sasha and I leapt to the ground to stretch our legs and get a closer look at the items for sale.

A few minutes later we heard the distinctive whine of Maria Dmitriyevna's voice as she marched back to the cart, "Ivan Osipovich! How could you have forgotten the flatbread my husband is so fond of. You know he likes to nibble on it with his tea."

The shopkeeper might have been napping, as he startled at the sound of his name. "But I did put some pieces out for you, right in plain sight. Why blame me if you have forgotten them?"

Sasha started walking toward a footpath that led along the riverbank, and I followed. We didn't go very far, and we could still hear the two arguing.

"I wish you had said something," Maria muttered.

"Why was it up to me?" He sounded a bit annoyed, and who could blame him. "If you didn't have a mind to remember, I would have said something, but I wasn't in the main building," Ivan Osipovich said in an apparent attempt to justify himself.

"Vanya! Sasha! Where are you going?" Maria Dmitriyevna screamed, just as we started up a small hill.

"We'll walk back, Mama. I bet we get back before you by taking this trail."

"Yes, well, you have strong, young legs. Vanya, would you prefer to ride back with us?" Her saccharine tone indicated a strong preference for that particular option.

We were already halfway up the hill. "No. No, thank you. I will walk with Sasha."

Once we reached the top of the rise, Sasha issued a challenge. "Let's go!" He removed his cap and started running, turning his slightly sweaty, flushed face to the wind. I caught up with him quickly. "This is one of my favourite things: running!"

I then realised this was Sasha's plan for arriving back before the cart. The breeze felt good, moving through the otherwise muggy air. After a few minutes, my face became flushed and sweaty as well.

"Will your father... be gone long?" I asked between gulps of breath.

"No. He doesn't usually stay at the Unzha River past St. Peter's Day at the end of the month. There isn't much to do there. He's just taking the air."

"Don't you ever go along with your father, Sasha?" I managed to keep up with him despite his superior muscles.

"Oh, I always go with him, but since you are here, I did not go this time."

"But why didn't you go? Are you trying to spare me?"

He pulled his cap back on, taming the black hair, which had scattered in all directions. Then he smiled and said, "I'm not sparing you at all, Vanya. I am very happy to stay with you. Of course, if it was just my mother, I would miss you, and this way I am very happy indeed." He smiled at me again.

We had reached another slight incline, and I slowed to a walk. Sasha realised he had gotten ahead, and he adjusted accordingly. Once I caught up with him, he continued in a more contemplative way, "After all, there is Unzha, Vetluga, Moscow and nothing to see but your own business, like a blind man. Everywhere you go all they speak of is lumber: *this* about lumber, *that* about the lumber, how much does it cost?, what is the charge to transport?, how many logs?, how many boards can be made from it? That's all you hear. Uncle Ivan is so like that, and that is all right because he wants to train me. And wherever we went, the woodsmen would immediately come up to us, at taverns, restaurants, and everywhere, it was all the same conversation." He seemed genuinely enthused to discuss this subject with me. "It's boring, I know, such as it is. Let's say you're a builder and you build nothing but churches, and not just churches, but only the eaves of churches; and you have travelled all over the world, but everywhere you go, you only look at church eaves. You never explore different people, how they live, how they think, pray, love. You don't look at trees, nor the colourful flowers of those places. All you ever looked at were the church eaves. I believe a person should be like a river or a mirror: life should be reflected upon, then accepted. And that way, like the Volga, you will have the sun and the clouds, the forests and high mountains, and cities with churches. Everything has to be exactly as it is, connected within itself. And the person who is hooked on one thing will be consumed by it and, even worse, totally self-interested, or it becomes god-like."

Oh, my goodness! Even this young man can go on and on about his opinions. I have to hope I shall never turn out this way. If there is such a thing as God, I pray that he grant me the gift of brevity. "That is, do you mean, like God?"

"Well, church-like, if you prefer. People who think and read about the same thing all the time find it difficult to understand anything else."

"But how is it there are clergymen who do not reject worldly possessions, even among your people? Bishop Innocent, for example."

"Of course there are, and, you know, I believe that it's wrong. It is impossible to be a good bishop, a good officer, a good merchant, knowing all you know. Because I tell you this, Vanya–and I envy you from the heart–none of us are prepared–not you, not me–and all you know is all you see. By the way, we are very close in age."

"Well, what would I know? They don't teach us that at school." However, some of what he said started to make sense. *All I knew was all I saw.*

"Yet, not knowing anything is preferable to knowing only one thing, if that's all you can understand."

I could hear the muffled rumbling of cart wheels down below, and from somewhere along the river came the sound of cursing and oars splashing.

Then I realised, "We haven't seen the rest of our party in a while," and I took a few more steps before my legs began to hurt. I saw a patch of grass by the trail ahead and sat there to give my body a rest.

"They must have called on the Loginovs along the way," Sasha explained as he sat beside me on the grass.

"You and I are the same age?" I asked as I looked across the Volga below, watching the shadows of storm clouds pass over the meadows on the opposite bank.

"How's that? We were born about a month apart. Larion Dmitriyevich told me."

Oh, no. Yet another person who knows my Stroop. Is there anyone in Russia he has not yet met? "That's interesting, Sasha. Do you know Larion Dmitriyevich?"

"Not really well. We only recently met. He seemed the sort of person you don't get to know very well at first meeting."

"Have you heard what happened, what they printed in the newspaper?" I had to wonder if the Sorokins were also mixed up in this horrid business.

"Yes, I have. We were still in St. Petersburg when it happened. Only I believe it was a lie, all made up. Such an injustice."

"A lie?" Perhaps there was another angle to this story after all.

"That the young lady did not kill herself. Larion Dmitrievich introduced me to her in the public garden. She was so wonderful. Then I also told Larion Dmitrievich, 'Mark my words, this young lady will come to a bad end.' I believe she'll become a blessed saint."

His logic escaped me. "But surely it's not possible to fire a gun *and* be the cause of a suicide."

"No, Vanya, but if someone gets truly upset about something that doesn't concern them, then no one else is responsible."

"So you blame Stroop for Ida Goldberg shooting herself?"

"Do you know why she shot herself?"

"I think you know, Sasha."

He took a moment to reply, "Because she loved him, and when she found him with Fyodor... well..."

"That's how it seems to me," I said, now feeling somewhat confused about the whole affair. In my mind I could see the red shirt, the tray with the empty decanter, and I recalled the scent of Stroop's *eau de cologne*.

Sasha stood up and began walking again, following the same path back toward the monastery. Not wanting to be left behind, and thankful for the short respite, I gathered myself up and followed after him. When I caught up, I could see his face looked totally blank, with no expression.

Off to the side of the hill, I saw the cart with Sergei, Ivan Osipovich, and Maria Dmitriyevna on the road climbing up to the level of our path. I looked at Sasha again, and his face appeared to be knotted into a scowl and somewhat angry.

"Sasha? Why haven't you responded?"

He looked at me with his irritated face and said with flat inno-cence, "Fyodor is a simple fellow, a peasant. I can't understand how anyone would take their own life because of him." Sasha looked down at the noisy cart and then back at me. "Perhaps Larion Dmitriyevich shouldn't have hired on a coachman for the horses or a doorman for the doors or sought out a physi-cian for a toothache. If he hadn't taken on Fyodor, it would have been necessary to –"

"Are you two waiting for us?" Maria Dmitriyevna shouted. Without realising it, we had reached the monastery. She dropped to the ground from the cart and collected various small bags and paper-wrapped cartons. Ivan Osipovich and Sergei stood watching a barking yard dog spin about.

~ П ~

The group's plan was to travel forty *verst* (similar to kilo-metres) up the Volga to assist a fellow priest with mass on the religiously important St. Peter's Day. While there, they were also planning to visit a distant relative who lived at the mon-astery's apiary. Another possible secondary destination was to have been Cheremshan, where Ivan Osipovich's daughters lived. However, the intended excursions were postponed until St. Ilyina's Day the last week of the following month. They would stay until the end of the celebration, and I was sup-posed to go with them.

The intention was to be that we would all gather together, the women from Cheremshan, the men from Unzha, and then I would return to St. Petersburg. I had no idea where I would live in the city as I had not communicated with anyone else the entire season.

A few days before we were supposed to have departed, as we sat in the cellar after supper drinking tea, the others went over the complicated plans at least ten times: who was going where, when, and how long each person would stay. Malanya trun-dled down the treacherous steps with two posts for me. This came as a surprise because I had not told anyone where I would be. One of the Kazanskys must have spoken to Stepan Stepanovich and obtained the postal address.

One letter was from Anna Nikolayevna asking if I could find a small *dacha* for 60 roubles because Nata ended up getting terribly melancholy, and she had been unable to endure the *dacha* near St. Petersburg. She also mentioned that their son Koka had departed for Notental, near Ganges, as a diversion for his grief over Ida Goldberg. Uncle Kostya and his brother Alexei remained in town conducting their business.

The other letter was from Koka, himself. In between gloomy phrases mourning "the death of this great woman, ruined by that villain," he informed me that at a nearby casino there were plenty of young ladies, and that he spent most of his days riding a bicycle, *etc.*, *etc.*

I had no clue why he chose me to express all his rambling thoughts. Was I the only person he knew with whom he could correspond? From what I remembered, I didn't even think he liked me that much.

"This is from the woman where I was staying in St. Petersburg. She is asking about a *dacha* she can rent near here."

"I believe the Germans' place is unoccupied. I had heard some people from Astrakhan were supposed to have rented it, but they never showed up, and it is quite close, not far from here," Maria Dmitriyevna informed me.

"Yes, if you please, could you inquire for me, and whether they will take 60 roubles, and how everything is in general." Not that I really wanted any of the Kazansky clan that close, but it might have been pleasant to see some different and familiar faces. Even the dreaded pouty ginger frog could prove to be a better companion than some of these tedious religious zealots.

"I will offer them 50, but don't you worry, Vanya, I will arrange everything."

I went back to my darkened room and sat for a long time at the window. Even though night had fallen, I did not light the lamp. My thoughts drifted back to St. Petersburg, the Kazanskys, Stroop and his beautiful apartment in Furshtadtskaya Street, and–for some inexplicable reason in particular–Fyodor as I had last seen him. The red silk shirt without a belt, the smile on his flushed face, which was not usually given to such colour, holding the tray with a decanter. I could picture it all without being there. All in a sudden, I had the urge to read from the volume of Shakespeare that Stroop had given me. I lit the lamp, opened the volume to *Romeo and Juliet* and attempted to read. I had no dictionary, and without Stroop I could only understand a bit of this and that. Then, some sort of flow that encompassed beauty and life suddenly overwhelmed me, as never before, perhaps something innate, unprecedented, or half-forgotten. It resurrected me, as it enveloped and embraced me with its passionate hands. Someone knocked softly at the door.

"Who's there?" I called out, half of me still in this dreamlike state.

"Me. May I come in?" The voice belonged to Maria Dmitriyevna.

"Please."

"I'm sorry. I know I interrupted you," she said as she stepped into the room. "I brought you a rosary. May I put it in your bag?"

I had never seen one like it. Back in the old church at home, a rosary consisted of beads on a cord. This device was flat and looked to be made from a leather strap with knots of twine in a ladder-like fashion all along it. Two triangular swatches hung at the apex.

Maria Dmitriyevna must have seen the bewilderment in my face. "These two tabs are symbolic of the two tablets given to Moses by God on Mt. Sinai."

"I see. Yes, please drop it into my bag. Thank you, Maria Dmitriyevna. Thank you very much."

She placed the rosary into my pack and slowly rose. "What was that you were reading?"

"Hmm?"

"I thought perhaps it was one of the manuscripts I gave you to read."

"Oh, no. Not that. It is a theatre work, from England."

"Ah, well. I had thought perhaps it was the manuscript. I could barely catch the words you recited because of the accent."

"Was I reading out loud?" If I was, I hadn't realised it.

"Yes, you were." She stepped to the box I used as a night stand. "I'll just leave this extra rosary for you here." And another of the strange pieces appeared. "Good night."

"Good night, Maria Dmitriyevna, and thank you."

She turned down the lamp and withdrew quietly, closing the door firmly behind her.

It astonished me how awake I felt. Around the room I observed the various religious icons in their cases, the lamp, the forged-metal trunk in the corner, the bed, the sturdy table under the window with its white curtain, through which I could see the garden and a star-filled sky. I closed my book and extinguished the lamp.

~ Π ~

The day for travel finally arrived, and I couldn't have been any happier to get away from the Sorokin compound. Not only had the heat gotten more distressing, my hands had been worked raw from the farming chores. These people did not believe in protective gloves, and the constant chafing of flesh on wooden farm tools brought my previously smooth skin to a state of near disrepair.

"So many Forget-Me-Nots by the river!" Maria Dmitriyevna exclaimed at frequent intervals as the wagon lumbered along a soggy marsh completely overgrown with the blue flowers. I had always had a fondness toward blue flowers for as long as I could remember. Birds peeked out from between tall stalks of river grass made nearly invisible by the awesome glittering, greenish wings of dragonflies.

At some point the cart slowed to a trot, and some of us jumped down to gather flowers. When Maria Dmitriyevna wasn't humming to herself, she prattled on–perhaps to me, perhaps not–seemingly intoxicated by the forest and the sun, the blue sky and flowers. I attempted to pay attention with tolerant sympathy as I looked upon the beaming face of this woman in her late thirties who seemed rejuvenated back to her adolescence.

"In Moscow, we had a wonderful garden in the Zamoskvorechye District. Apples, lilac roses, and in the corner was the well and a raspberry bush. We never went anywhere in the summer, so I used to spend the whole day in the garden. I even put up my preserves in the garden... I love it here, Vanya, to be able walk around barefoot on ground hot like a griddle or to bathe in the cooling stream. In the water you can see your entire body, golden rays of the sun reflecting off the running water. You plunge in and open your eyes there, and everything is green, green, and you see the little fish skim by. Then you lie down on the hot sand to dry, the wind blows. How nice!"

She paused to inhale, stretch her arms out fully, and smile at me.

"And it is better as you lie there by yourself, no girlfriends, nobody. And it isn't true what old women say about the body being sinful. There is no sin in flowers and beauty; there is no sin in washing; there is no such sin at all. Didn't the Lord create all of this: the water, trees, and the body? It's only a sin if you resist the will of the Lord. When, for example, someone is given to something not allowed, something they are bursting to do, and it is not permitted, that is a sin!"

In between breaths she stopped to pick a few more flowers. "And you will need to hasten, Vanya, I can't tell you enough! As a good housewife stores cabbage and cucumbers in a timely fashion, knowing she will not be able to get them later, you and I, Vanya, must feast our eyes and love and breathe while we still can! How much time do we have? Youth never lasts very long, and every minute that passes will never come again. You must always keep that in mind. That way everything will be twice as sweet, like a baby just opening its eyes for the first time, or an old man closing his for the last."

Oh, my. How maudlin. She touched on the highs and lows, the good and the bad. Every irreplaceable minute ticking by made me wonder if this life is even worth the effort. Perhaps these Old Believers only saw our existence as a means of postponing suffering.

We had fallen behind the wagon, and in the distance I could hear the voices of our party. I was also aware of buzzing flies, the smell of the grass, the pungent marsh and the sweet flowers. It was so hot.

Ivan Osipovich halted the horses to allow us to catch up. I helped Maria Dmitriyevna back to her seat. Even with her sparkling dark eyes and her loose-fitting black dress and white scarf, she looked pale from fatigue and heat. I sat next to her with a slightly hunched back as we examined the flowers we had picked.

"It's all the same to me, Vanya"–she confided as the cart began to move off again–"what I believe for myself, and what I say to you because I feel that you have an innocent soul."

After a sharp turn in the road, a vast field opened before us with many grey, timeworn houses facing into it. Most appeared to be dilapidated sheds without windows or with windows only on the upper floors. There was no apparent street. No people could be seen, and only barking dogs raced towards our cart, which filled the air with dust as we approached the abbey.

~ Π ~

Following the mass, the Sorokins and I set out to visit Elder Leonty, who lived at the apiary half a *verst* from the abbey. We walked hastily through a shady grove into a small clearing where, among the tall grass and flowers, I could hear an invisible stream flowing in a wooden drain.

Maria Dmitriyevna grasped my hand and informed me, "You see, Elder Leonty moved from the Great Russian Church to The True Church a long time ago, that would be about 30 years now, and even then he was no longer young. But he's a sturdy old man, a bit zealous, perhaps. He stood for trial four times in court and spent two years in Suzdal, the monastery prison. He fasts like it's Great Lent all the time, let alone how he prays. Like a mad man. Like a spinning wheel! And he has the gift of foresight... You do too, Vanya, so don't tell him directly that you are Orthodox. He might not like to hear that."

"Perhaps I should tell him. That way he could begin to instruct me."

"No, I think it best if you don't tell him..."

"Yes, well, all right," I replied, a bit absent-mindedly. I looked with curiosity at the low hut with stalks of flower-laden rose mallow all around. A grey-haired old man in a white shirt and blue trousers wearing a small pointed black cap sat on a stump near the door of the building. He sported a long, narrow beard and he had lively, merry eyes.

"As he arrived, this priest," the old man started speaking as we approached, as if we had been present for the beginning of the story. "I was upstairs. He went right to the table and opened the Gospel. 'What luck,' he says, 'yours is the correct version, otherwise I would be compelled to take it. However, I shall take away the pictures and this manuscript without fail.' I had hung portraits of Semyon Denisov, Peter Filippov and some of the others on the wall. But I was not yet old, still healthy, and I said, 'That's what you say, Father, but I will not allow you to take anything away.' The Deacon, who had been drinking the wine, moaned quite a bit, but he said, 'Stop it, Father.' The priest threw me on the bed and was after pouring tea out of a saucer over me–to baptise me, I presume–but I was strong. I resisted, and he desisted. 'Good-bye,' he says, 'I shall have a talk with you another time,' and I went to escort him out, but he grabbed me and shoved me down the hill."

Here is yet another who went on and on about personal beliefs. After listening to him recite, by rote, how he had been with a religious sect, the Nekrasovs, in Turkey and how they tried to kill him, how a judge sent him to Suzdal, and so forth, my focus began to wander. He said something about how everywhere he had gone, it was his cross and religious relics that saved him. While he prattled on, he brought out of the house, squatting down to get through the low doorway, a hollow cross with an inscription in the bronze base: "The relics of St. Peter, Metropolitan Bishop of Moscow and miracle worker; St. Blessed Princess Olga, Fevronia of Murom; St. Jonah, the Prophet; St. Blessed Prince Dmitry; our Venerable Mother Mary of Egypt."

While the others cooed over the cross like it was a new baby, I peeked inside the little hut through the window. I could see icons lined up like an army regiment, the reddish light from the ceremonial lamps and candles. There were dusty, leather-bound books piled on the windowsill and the table, and a bare bench with a log at the head.

Elder Leonty had walked up and put a hand on my shoulder, which startled me. Then, looking rather out-of-place with his merry eyes, said to me, in a singsong manner, "Be strong, son, and remain in the True Faith because what could be loftier than the True Faith itself? It masks all sins, and in the house of eternal light you shall dwell. Eternal is the light of our Lord Jesus. You must love him more than anything or anyone. What is eternal, what is everlasting and as resplendent as Paradise, and the salvation of your soul? A flower might captivate or tempt you, but tomorrow it shall wither. Tomorrow you may fall in love with a man, but the next day, he will die. Bright eyes will fade, ruddy cheeks turn yellow. Your hair, your teeth will all fall out, and in the end, all you are is worm fodder. Walking corpses, that is the fate of all Humanity."

Again, more irretrievable minutes ticked away, leaving me to wonder if it is even worth growing old, just knowing how things shall end: ashes to ashes, dust to dust, and I shall be nothing more than tasty food for worms crawling through the undying earth. And then I remembered what Stroop had told me about the easing of religious restrictions. "But won't it be easier now? Your church will be able to grow. You will be able to pray and have your services openly." I attempted to hearten the old fellow.

"Do not pursue what is easy, but rather what is difficult! Nations perish from ease, freedom, and wealth. However, in austere suffering, one can save his faith. The enemy of mankind is sly and cunning, and we must test every merciful condition to determine from whence it came."

As we walked back to the abbey from the apiary, I asked Maria Dmitriyevna, "How did Elder Leonty grow to be so embittered?"

"Consider this: Are people you love guilty of a sin because they die?" Maria Dmitriyevna asked in return. "And furthermore, I would love even harder if I knew that tomorrow I was condemned to death."

"Love everyone and everything you can," Sasha contributed. He had been silent the whole day. "Because you can't give your heart to just one thing or else that one thing will consume it."

His mother rolled her eyes. "Here is yet another philosopher," and she gave him a playful swat on the back of his head.

"What? Am I lacking in brains?"

"And how is it he did not recognise that you are Orthodox? I told you he had the gift of sight, and perhaps he foresaw, my dear, that you will eventually arrive at the True Faith," Maria Dmitriyevna, said with a honeyed look on her face.

~ Π ~

The bedroom I shared with Sasha back at the abbey was lit by a single lamp and almost completely dark. Through the window I could see deep-red, and up above, the yellowing sky of sunset hovering over a black pine forest beyond the clearing.

Sasha stood at the window, his image darkened by the reddish evening. He began, "It is difficult to relate everything together. As one of our folk said, 'After the theatre, how you will read the canon to Jesus? It is easier to kill a person.' Sure enough! We can kill, steal, or commit adultery under any faith, but to understand *Faust* and earnestly pray with a rosary is unthinkable. Or at least God-knows-what, the Devil's torment. And yet if a person resists sin and acts within the rules, but does not believe in their necessity or that they bring salvation, that is worse than not fulfilling them, just having faith. But how can you have faith when you do not have a faith? How do you know what you know, not remember what you remember? And that is impossible to judge. That is wise. I shall obey the rules, that's easy, a trifle. But who made you the judge? As long as our church does not abolish them, all the rules must be enforced. We should shun the secular arts, observe all fasts, and not be treated by infidel doctors. Only the elders in the forest can keep the old Orthodox Church. What should I call those that are not in a position, and in a position, whom we don't need to consider, and they don't count? I believe that only a handful of our people shall be saved while the rest of the world lolls about in sin. And if I don't believe that, how can I be regarded as an Old Believer? Likewise, every other faith and lifestyle judges all outsiders harshly. If you accept them all simultaneously, then you cannot be a true believer of any of them."

At that point in time, I had not yet read Karl Marx's treatise that contained "*Die Religion ist das Opium des Volkes,*" but thinking back on Sasha's tirade against non-believers and infidel doctors, I realised that faith can be a comforting balm to those who cannot think for themselves.

Fearing a further torrent, instead of responding, I just sat on the bed in the darkness. Unfortunately, after a few breaths, he started up again.

"But perhaps it is understandable and obvious to you that we are trapped in our beliefs, our lives, our faith, our rituals, and our people because you may witness these things in a way we cannot. No, not really, or else it's only one part of you, but not the main part. Please understand that to Papa and our elders, you have always been a stranger, an outsider. There is nothing you can do about it. No matter how much I love or respect you, Vanya, I still feel there is something within you that is unyielding and confusing. Our fathers and our grandfathers lived in different ways of thinking and knowing—and we ourselves could never dream of achieving what you have. Certainly anything unusual reveals itself eventually, and only wishing for it to happen won't make a difference."

When Sasha stopped again, all I could hear was very faint singing from the chapel through its open door.

We both listened in thought for a while and then I asked, "And what about Maria Dmitriyevna?"

"My mother? What about her?"

"What does she think? Does she go along with the others?" I thought back to her soliloquy in the orchard.

"Who knows? She is devout. What else can I say?"

"She has been very good to me."

"Yes. My mother is very good to everyone, but she is not very imaginative," Sasha said as he closed the window.

As I prepared myself to sleep, I thought about this revelation from Sasha. His family sees me as an outsider, a foreigner. This made me laugh to myself because until I arrived in St. Petersburg, I was just like them, a country boy, provincial and blinkered. Life in the city has exposed me to new ways of being and thinking. I was no longer the naïve bumpkin who suffocated on the cultural sophistication of St. Petersburg. How foreign I would seem to my neighbours back in my home town now.

These Old Believers saw me as someone who considered himself better than them. Much like Jonathan Swift's character, Doctor Gulliver, I have landed on several remote islands where I felt quite out of place. But everywhere he went, Gulliver learned new things from his hosts. Perhaps there would be lessons for me to discover here as well.

The mattress we shared shuddered as Sasha sat down next to me. As I turned to look at him in the dim light, he placed his hand on my leg, and I smiled. He brought his face close to mine–I could smell his pungent sweat quite clearly–and he kissed me gently on the cheek. My whole body went rigid.

Before I could thaw, he had turned and lain down, his head near where my feet would be. "God be with you, Vanya."

As I attempted to adjust myself into a comfortable sleeping position parallel to Sasha, I heard him whisper to himself, "Now, as I lay myself down for sleep..."

~ Π ~

By the time we returned to the Sorokin compound at the monastery along the Volga, Anna Nikolayevna and Nata had taken the Germans' *dacha* for 50 roubles, as arranged by Maria Dmitriyevna.

Soon after, the Sorokins decided to open their doors to all the Old Believers in the area to celebrate the end of the Fast of the Assumption, the day that Holy Mother Mary ascended to Heaven. Tables had been set up all around and carts carrying celebrants arrived almost non-stop. As each new group appeared, there was cheering and hugging and kissing. Unfamiliar people, children and animals ran about creating all sorts of unpleasant noises and smells. Maria Dmitriyevna assisted Malanya to keep food and drink supplied to all.

The guests ate, drank, and sang merrily. On the tables covered with white cloths stood decanters of Madeira and brandy, and next to them companies of flies crawled up and down the glasses or landed on the crumbs of bread. Some of the flies clung to the whitewashed walls to digest their meals.

Due to the sultry heat, men sat shirtless with their jackets, waistcoats, and sacraments flung over the backs of their chairs. When they weren't eating, they argued, laughed, or belched, all rather loudly. From each table rose the smell of raspberries, sweetcakes, wine, and sweat.

The sun had just reached the point where it shone through the door of the hall, illuminating the glass enclosure for the ceremonial lamps and candles, filling the room with a shiny iridescence. The canaries chirped passionately from the painted cages, adding to the cacophony.

At one point, Maria Dmitriyevna stopped next to me and said, "Vanya, please go down to the cellar to see if we have any more kvass," and she toddled off to fill a newcomer's glass. Near the top of the stairs, I passed the table where Anna Nikolayevna and Nata sat. Both clasped handkerchiefs drenched with per-spiration, and their faces dripped with more moisture.

Stepping out of the way of the running dogs and children, I tapped Nata on the shoulder and nodded my head in the di-rection of the stairs to the cellar. Even though I detested the whine of her voice and the agony of her emotional effluence, she possessed information I required. Nata excused herself from the table and followed me. Auntie Anna looked the oppo-site way.

As we navigated through the throng, I heard bits of conversa-tions: "Well, judge for yourself! I ordered him to answer the telegram from Samara, but he wrote not one word!"; "First, go to the cellar and douse it with spirits, blow it dry, leave it for a day and then cook it over oak bark. Very tasty indeed!"; "For Ascension, Father Vasyli from Gromovsky gave an excellent speech: 'Blessed are the peacemakers. Because of you the trustees of the Chubykinskoy alms-house did not ask for a reconciliation of accounts, and they forgave all debts!' I couldn't stop laughing..."; "I said 35 roubles, and he gave me only 15..."; "Blue. So blue with pink streaks..."

When we reached the top of the stairs to the cellar, Nata turned to me, "Do you like this life, Vanya?"

"Not exactly, but there are worse things, you know." I looked at her freckly face, but her eyes seemed focused on something farther away.

"I can't think of any." The back of her grey, silk skirt had gotten caught on a stone by the archway, and she worked at pulling it free.

Once she liberated herself, I started down the old brick stairs. "Be careful," I warned, "these stones can be tricky."

"I think I know how to walk down stairs, Vanya," she snorted. Fate intervened after a few steps when one of her shoes slipped on a worn-smooth section, and she tumbled down to the cellar floor with a, "Humph!"

My first thought was to make fun of her misfortune; however, living with these Old Believers had taught me a few things about providence. "Here, let me help you," I offered as I extended a hand.

"Thank you, but I think I can handle this part myself." She pressed a hand against the cold stone wall to steady herself. Her nose wrinkled at the assortment of appalling smells. "What is this place used for? Penance? Phew!" She waved a hand in front of her nose.

"Most of the time it's a storeroom, or a sprouting cellar, but during the hot period we eat our supper down here." I walked to the stacks of barrels to look for kvass.

"You *eat* down here?" Nata turned her head this way and that, pinching her freckly nose with her freckly fingers.

I picked up one of the dusty vats of kvass and handed it her. "Here, take this up to Maria Dmitriyevna, please."

She placed her lower arms under the container and started back to the stairs. "No wonder these people are so peculiar. This is where they *eat*!"

Nata managed to reach the top without incident, and I carried another vat upstairs. Maria Dmitriyevna didn't even acknowledge our contributions, as she was busy ordering Malanya to refill the pitchers with the kvass we had brought up from below. I walked to one of the empty benches away from the crowd, in the shade of a birch tree, and motioned for Nata to follow me.

"Let's sit here, Nata. I would like to speak with you." I sat and she followed.

"I will sit with you, perhaps, but what do you want to talk about?" Her brow furrowed as if she knew what I wanted to discuss.

From where we sat you could see the basilica, which had fallen into disrepair. The dilapidated wooden gates stood open, and the melodic voices of painters and builders could be heard singing old secular songs that the travelling priest had previously forbade. "Only righteous music in a righteous building!" he had admonished on more than one occasion. Thick, spiky bushes obscured the vestibule, but every word was clearly audible in the evening air. In counterpoint, a herd of cows lowed as they walked along a nearby path.

"Well," Nata scowled, "what is it you wish to speak about?"

"I don't know," I began. My mind had drifted as I listened to the hearty chants. I couldn't remember the last time I felt happy enough to sing like that. "It might be difficult or unpleasant for you to think about." I looked toward the church, away from Nata.

"You probably want to speak about the suicide affair," she said after a bit of a pause.

"Yes," I looked back at her. "If there is any way you can explain it to me, please do so." I needed to know what happened in Stroop's apartment for my own peace of mind.

"You are quite mistaken if you think that I know more than others." Nata turned her head away. "I only know that Ida Goldberg shot herself; however, the reasons for her action are unknown to me."

"You were there at the time it happened?"

"I was," she nodded, "but not half an hour like they said in the newspaper. Perhaps ten minutes, seven of which I stood waiting in the hall by myself."

"Did she shoot herself in front of you?"

"No. When I heard the shot, I ran down the hall and opened the door to his rooms."

"And she was already dead?"

Nata just nodded instead of giving a verbal answer, then dropped her head to her chest.

The singers in the church prolonged the phrase, *"Let my prayer arise!"*

"Go to the Devil! What do you think you're doing?! Damn you!" A woman's voice cried out from the vestibule, "Aaah!"

I could hear rustling noises, as if an invisible assailant continued his assault in silence. "Aaah!" she cried out again, but at a higher pitch, and the spiky bushes began to tremble, even though no wind blew. I wanted to investigate this disturbance, but I needed to finish speaking with Nata first.

"The vesper sacrifice!" the chorus from within concluded in pleasing harmony.

With a bit of a tear in one eye, Nata faced me again, rummaging up each memory as it resurfaced. "On the table sat a decanter or a siphon–something made of glass–and a bottle of cognac. There was a young man in a red shirt on a chair by the same table. Stroop was seated on the leather sofa to the right, and Ida was sitting, her head thrown back in the chair, and on the desk –"

"She was already dead?"

My interposing question disrupted her, and she took a breath to recoup. "Yes, it seemed like she was already dead. As soon as I walked in, he said to me, 'Why are *you* here?' which, I guess, was a proper question as I did not have an appointment. When I just stood there dumbfounded, he prompted me, 'For your happiness, for your peace of mind, go away. Go away *now*, please?' The young man stood up, and I noticed that he was not wearing a belt. His red, flushed face was very beautiful, and his hair was somewhat curly. I thought he might have been drunk. And then Stroop said: 'Fyodor, show the young lady out'."

"Thy will be done," sang the people in the church. It sounded like the couple hidden in the bushes near the vestibule had reconciled, as I could hear soft murmuring without shouting. The woman seemed to be crying tenderly.

"All the same," I offered, "it is still awful."

"Awful?!" echoed Nata, "For me it is even worse!" I could not believe how self-centred she was being. "I really love that man." She started weeping openly. Suddenly, Nata appeared to have grown old before my eyes. This somewhat flabby girl with tousled red hair, whose vulgar mouth started to swell, had so much blood rushing to her face that her freckles began to fuse into solid brownish spots.

"Do you really love Larion Dmitriyevich?"

She nodded and swiped at her puffy eyes. Suddenly, she stopped sniffling and looked at me clear-eyed. "Are you still corresponding with him, Vanya?" How she can turn her emotions on and off as necessary.

"No, he quit the apartment in St. Petersburg, and I don't have his new address." As if I would have provided it to her even if I did have it.

"But couldn't you find it?" The light had started to return to her coppery eyes.

"What? So that I can conduct your business for you by keeping up correspondence with him?" I could not believe her cheek. But perhaps I would have asked the same question if I were in her situation.

"No, I suppose not. Never mind." She looked away as the tears began to flow again.

Appearing out of the bushes came a man in a jacket and a cap, and when he got closer, he bowed to me. It was Sergei.

After he had gone far enough away, Nata whispered loudly, "Who was that?"

"Sergei, the eldest Sorokin boy." I laughed to myself, realising he had been the one tormenting the squealing young lady in the bushes.

"He was probably only the hero of that little story we heard earlier."

"What story?"

"Over in the bushes by the vestibule. Didn't you hear anything?"

"I heard a woman crying, but that means nothing to me."

She stared hard at me with her coppery eyes afire.

~ П ~

Once it started to get dark, the guests began to leave, presumably to get back to their own homes before night fell. Fortunately for me, Nata and Anna Nikolayevna were among the first to depart. As much as I detested conversing with the ginger frog and her spectrum of soppy emotions, she did provide me with some valuable information. As much as I wanted to believe that she was the one who shot Ida Goldberg, from what she told me, it sounded more and more like a genuine suicide.

As I helped Maria Dmitriyevna collect the dirty plates and glasses, I almost tripped over the foot of a person leaning against a wall in the courtyard. He wore a white suit with a summer uniform cap that had drifted down from the top of his slightly bald head to cover one eye. One of his hands curled under his chin, the other lodged against his upturned nose. The visible bristles of the reddish beard caught my attention because that particular colour was fairly rare. His figure was slight but fit, and I realised it could be only one person: my Greek teacher.

"Are you really here, Daniel Ivanovich?" I said in amazement, forgetting even to say hello first.

His head tilted up to meet mine, and a trail of dried wine led down from his mouth. "As you can see, Vanya! But why are you so surprised to see me? You are here, and you are also from St. Petersburg." One of his eyes remained partially closed.

"Yes, well, but why haven't I seen you here before?" I was surprised but also glad to see a familiar face. Was the whole city of St. Petersburg about to descend on the compound? It wouldn't have startled me if my schoolmates, Nikolayev and Shpilevsky, popped up out of nowhere, not to mention my beloved Stroop.

"That is understandable as I just arrived yesterday. Are you here with your family?" asked the teacher as he adjusted himself and his clothing. He pulled a red-bordered pocket square from the jacket and began dabbing at his sweaty scalp. "Can you sit with me a minute?"

I placed the collection of plates and glasses on a nearby table and sat on the ground next to Daniel Ivanovich. "They're not exactly my family. It's Anna Nikolayevena and her niece, Nata, who have taken a *dacha* nearby. I'm here on my own with the Sorokins. Have you heard of them?"

"I have not yet had the pleasure of their acquaintance." He belched and looked about at the courtyard and the forest across the Volga. "It is quite nice here. Very nice, indeed. I have taken the small, blue cottage down the lane. It's barely big enough for little me," he giggled, "but..."–he swept the vista with the arm that was not holding him up–"the Volga... the orchard... and such..." He started to nod off again.

"But what about your kitten and your thrush? Did you bring them with you?"

"No... I'm going to be travelling for quite a while, you know..." He looked at me, and then back at the river. "I received a small inheritance unexpectedly, and now I'm taking a long overdue vacation, Vanya. For the longest time I have wanted to see the likes of Athens, Alexandria, and Rome. I will set out in the autumn, when it won't be as hot wandering around the southern regions. For now, I'm just travelling along the Volga, stopping where I like, with only a small suitcase, and three or four of my favourite books."

"That's wonderful, Daniel Ivanovich! I am so happy for you." I thought of my own pitiful, non-existent inheritance and tried not to feel envious. I wanted to travel, too. I wanted to see those places. I wanted to learn about other peoples.

"Now, in Rome, Pompeii, and parts of Asia," he went on, "the most interesting excavations and new literary works of the ancients have recently been found there." The Greek teacher's eyes flashed and gleamed as he took off his cap and placed it on the ground next to him. As he went on, at length and with enthusiasm, about his dreams and plans, I started to feel sorry for myself. He had the freedom to roam about at his whimsy, while I had to rely upon virtual strangers for my daily bread. Even though he had a shining, shimmering vitality, I now looked upon my small, bald Greek teacher's ugly face and felt sad.

"Yes, yes. It all sounds very interesting. Very interesting, indeed," I droned absent-mindedly when he finally stopped talking.

"And you're planning to be here until the end of autumn?" Daniel Ivanovich asked somewhat abruptly.

"Probably," I responded in a despondent tone. It wasn't like I had many options available to me. No one wanted the orphan boy with the thin, arched eyebrows. "I will attend the fair in Lower Novgorod and then return to St. Petersburg, I guess." I confess I felt ashamed at having to share these trifling affairs after hearing about his wonderful plans.

"Are you satisfied with that, Vanya?" he asked. "These Sorokins, are they... interesting people?"

"There are quite simple, good and kindly." Uncharitable thoughts suddenly filled my head as I realised these people were no more than acquaintances to me. "I really miss you, Daniel Ivanovich. Really, I do!" He looked at me with quizzical eyes. "There is no one here, you know, who has been able to inspire my enthusiasm. If only one person could just under-stand and share the slightest stirring of my soul." I blurted suddenly, "Not here, nor, perhaps, in St. Petersburg."

He looked at me keenly with those bright eyes. "Smurov," he began, somewhat solemnly, "you already have a friend who is capable of appreciating the greatest expressions of emotion, and the spirit, who will always receive you with compassion and love." A small tear formed in a corner of one eye.

"Thank you, Daniel Ivanovich"–I smiled and extended my hand to him–"I feel blessed to hear that from you," and I felt happy for the first time in quite a while.

"It is my pleasure." He returned the smile. "Especially because what I said was not about me."

"No? Who were you speaking of, then?" It certainly sounded like a sincere expression of his feelings.

"Larion Dimitriyevich, of course."

"Stroop?" No one could have been more surprised by this than me.

"Yes... Now, don't interrupt me. I know Larion Dmitrievich very well. I saw him soon after the unfortunate incident with the young lady, and I can swear with absolute certainty that he was as much to blame as you were." My thin eyebrows raised at hearing that. "It would be similar to blaming me, for example, if I drowned myself just because *you* have blond hair. Of course, Larion Dmitrievich really doesn't care what others say about him, but he did express regret that some of the people who are dear to him–you included"–he levelled a finger at me–"could change your opinion of him so quickly." Perhaps I did judge him hastily, after all. "Please keep all of this in mind, as well as that he is now in Munich, at the Four Seasons Hotel."

All of a sudden I began to suspect that my Greek teacher showed up here with some intention. "Well, please understand that I have not judged him, and I certainly do not need his address. If you've come here just for that purpose, then I am afraid you have wasted your time, Daniel Ivanovich."

"My friend, and I hope we are still friends," his cocked head and half-smile were quite endearing. "I'm afraid you are acting a bit too arrogant for your own good." He pointed at his left side with his right hand. "Do you think this old man stopped at Vasilsursk on his way from St. Petersburg to Rome just to give you, Vanya Smurov, Stroop's address?" The hand that pointed to his chest returned to the ground after brushing aside the air. "I didn't even know you were here. You're upset, you're unwell, and I–like a good doctor, and a mentor–am pointing out what you are wanting: the kind of life that you desire for yourself as embodied by our friend Stroop, and that's all."

He attempted to stand, but in his weakened state, it took a few tries. The hand used for support slipped down the wall, his knees buckled. I reached over to offer some assistance, but he held out his arm, as if pushing me away, indicating he would prefer to achieve an upright posture on his own. Much like a marionette with elastic strings, he made a few humorous attempts before he was finally able to stand on his own. It took a bit of fortitude to keep from laughing out loud at him, as he looked quite the buffoon. Once he appeared to be stable, I

Part Two

handed him his hat. Daniel Ivanovich snatched it from my hand, positioned the hat upon his head at a jaunty angle, patted down the dust from his white suit, and sauntered off to wherever he happened to be staying. I just sat there and watched him depart, reflecting on the invaluable lesson he had attempted to impart.

"Don't just sit there, lazy boy!" Maria Dmitriyevna snarled, "You are supposed to be helping clear the tables, not gathering wool!" She grabbed the pile of dishes and glasses I had collected and strode back across the courtyard.

~ Π ~

"My! How well-made you are, Vanya!"

I had gone down to the riverbank to bathe in the morning. My feet had sunk into the sandy soil, and I was just about to bend over to cup some water in my hands, when Sasha appeared. Even though he was muscular, he had short legs and was a bit plump. He began to undress as well.

What an enigma. At the abbey in Unzha he went on and on about righteousness and then kissed me. Here he told me I was 'well-made.' In some ways, he seemed more confused than me. It was comforting to know that at least one person found me appealing.

I hadn't thought about my appearance in quite some time. Looking down at the rippling reflection in the water, I attempted to stand motionless to get a better look. Compared to Sasha, my body seemed taller, more flexible, with narrow hips and long, slender legs, tanned from so much exposure to the sun. My hair had grown, with an abundance of curls circling my thin neck. Even my face seemed thinner, less round, making my eyes appear bigger than they were.

Suddenly, it seemed so silly, standing there gawking at myself. I smiled one more time at the slightly-obscured mirrored vision and then reached into the cold Volga and drew up handfuls of water to moisten my armpits and the crown of my head.

Across the river, on the shore opposite, I could see a group of children bathing, shrieking, running about on the beach and through the water. Here and there, piles of red shirts and undergarments. On the hill above them, sitting on bright green well-trimmed grass under white willows, I glimpsed more children and some other people closer to our age. The idyllic arrangement of their pale-pink bodies evoked a painting of paradise, in the dream-like fashion of German artist Hans Thoma.

When I began to swim like a fish, I experienced an almost-passionate joy as my body cut through the cold, deep water and rapid turns. Up at the warmer surface, foam had formed. After a few minutes, I was exhausted, and I floated on my back, looking up and seeing only the bright sun in the sky. I remained motionless, not moving my hands, and not knowing where I was headed.

Loud screams from the beach roused me from my trance. When I looked up, the noise seemed to be coming from the crowd of people up on the hill under the white willows. They started pulling on their clothes as they raced down toward the river. "They found him!" people cried, "They found him and they've pulled him out!"

I couldn't make sense of what they were yelling until I heard a strange mechanical noise behind me. When I turned round I saw a river dredger headed toward me.

Some of the people had reached the bank, and I navigated my way to land and up toward them. "What is going on?" I called once I got close enough.

"He had drowned," one fellow stopped to tell me as the rest of the crowd ran past us. "He got caught in some logs, last spring, and I believe he was unable to swim."

A woman in a red dress with a white headscarf came running down the side of the hill, crying loudly. By that time, the dredger had pulled ashore, and the pilot had carried a body and laid it upon a bed of reeds. When the woman reached the place where the body lay, she fell face down on the sand and began to cry even louder, wailing in agony and grief.

"It's Arina, his mother," I heard people whisper.

"Remember, I told you about him," Sergei had appeared from somewhere.

It was the first time I had seen a dead body, and I looked with horror upon the swollen, slimy corpse, the face already deformed. Although he had no clothing, the boots had remained on his feet. It was disgusting and terrible in the bright, honest sunlight. Noisy and curious children, whose pale pink bodies could be seen through their unbuttoned shirts, began to circle round.

"He was an only son, and all he wanted to do was become a monk. Three times he ran off, but they kept turning him away because he was too young. They even beat him, but to no avail. Most children buy spice cakes with their kopeks, but he spent all his pocket coins on candles. Then, around Easter, this girl shows up. Everyone else thought she was a tart, but he did not understand anything. How could he understand? A week later he went to swim with his mates and he drowned. Only 16 years old..."

That's probably what Sergei told me, but I had been so traumatised from seeing the corpse that his story came to me somewhat garbled, as through water.

"Vanya!" cried the woman in a piercing, shrill voice, rising and falling over the swollen, slimy body of her son on the bed of reeds over and again. "Vanya!"

A dreadful horror fell over me when she screamed the boy's name–it being the same as mine–and I swam back across the Volga and ran up the hill, stumbling, clawing on bushes and nettles. I never looked back, as if being pursued by demons. My heart beat like never before, and the clamour in my brain didn't stop until I reached the Sorokin's garden, where I found strange comfort in the reddened apples on the sparsely planted trees, the dark forest on the calm Volga, chirping grasshoppers, and the smell of honey and balsam.

~ П ~

We have muscles and ligaments in our human body that cannot be observed unless they pulsate! The words of Stroop resonated in my mind. I kept seeing the image of the boy's pale, bloated body lying in the rushes by the river. Vanya! his mother screamed. Vanya! How it haunted me.

I spent the rest of the day alone in the little room. Everyone else went about their everyday chores, and only Malanya appeared with small meals and tea for me.

By the time the sun had set I was finally able to think about something other than the boy's empty shell. I lit the lamp and stood near the mirror. The flickering reflection showed my thin face, now terribly pale, the delicate eyebrows and grey eyes, the bright red mouth, and curly hair, all atop my thin neck. It horrified me.

I was not sure how long I stood mesmerised by my own spectre-like image, but some time late in the evening Maria Dmitriyevna entered the room without making a sound. She quietly shut the door tightly behind her. I was too stunned to be surprised that she would visit at such a late hour, but then I thought it might be good to have some comforting human interaction.

"What does it mean? What does it all mean?" Like a foolish, scared child, I cried out and rushed to her. "The sunken cheeks will grow pale, the slimy flesh bloats, worms will eat out my eyes, all the joints of my lovely frame will come apart! And there are muscles and ligaments in our human body that cannot be observed unless they pulsate! Everything will slip away and perish! I don't know anything, I haven't seen anything, but I want... I want... I'm not that insensitive, I'm not some kind of heartless stone, and now I realise how truly beautiful I am. It is terrifying! Terrifying! Who will rescue me?"

Maria Dmitriyevna, looked upon me with a little smile and a slight tilt of her head. Again, I was not surprised by her reaction.

"Vanya, my dove," she cooed, "I am so sorry for you, so sorry..." She stepped closer.

All of a sudden I was petrified, and I couldn't explain why. I felt truly alien.

"I wondered when this would happen. It is God's will. The time has come." She turned the lamp down, faced me and then clutched my torso.

My body went rigid with the unfamiliar feeling. It was almost as if I was outside of myself, watching what was going on with no control.

She began to kiss my mouth, my eyes, and my cheeks, all the more pressing against my chest. Suddenly I came to my senses and started to feel excessively warm and clammy. I felt awkward and cramped, and I struggled to break free from the strumpet's embrace. In a voice I had never used before, deep, resonant and menacing, I quietly repeated, "Maria Dmitriyevna, Maria Dmitriyevna," and I pushed her away. "What are you doing? You mustn't let this happen."

She pulled me close and started softly kissing my cheeks, my mouth, and my eyes again. "Vanya, my dove, my joy..."

"Let me go, you disgusting woman!" I shouted as I struggled to break free from her grasp again. The door to the room stuck as I pulled at it, but after a few panicky attempts, it finally let go. I dashed out, slammed the door closed behind me and just kept running until I was out of the compound.

~ Π ~

I ran for a while along the banks of the Volga, not knowing what to do next. I couldn't go back to the Sorokins now, and I had no way to get to Munich to be with Stroop. The two Kazanskys here, Nata and Auntie Anna, would be a port of last resort.

When I passed the small blue cottage, there was a lamp visible through the drawn muslin curtain. Before knocking, I attempted to calm myself before invading my Greek teacher's private time.

In an attempt to draw as little attention as possible, I knocked gently on the door. A book slammed shut, feet shuffled, the door opened, and there stood Daniel Ivanovich in bedroom slippers and a dressing gown over his undergarments. "Smurov," he pronounced as if I owed him a pile of roubles that he never expected to see again.

"Daniel Ivanovich, I am so very sorry to disturb you during your private hours, but I must speak to you. May I please come in?"

He held the door partially closed, suggesting that my company might have been unwelcome. "If you are here to apologise for your juvenile behaviour from evening last, just know that it might take some time for those wounds to heal. Please return to your Sorokins now, and we shall discuss this matter at another time." He started to close the door. "A good night to you, Smurov."

"No, wait, Daniel Ivanovich!" I whispered loudly. He re-opened the door a bit. "Something terrible has happened and I cannot return to the Sorokins. Please let me come in and explain. Please."

As I stood there, I observed his facial features slowly relax until I could recognise my kindly old Greek teacher once more. "Something terrible, you say?" A hint of a smile curved his lip, and the door opened farther. "Yes, yes. Come in. By all means."

He turned the lamp up a bit and then sat on the only chair in the room. "What has happened that is so terrible, Vanya?"

I stood before him and recounted the day's events, from the dredging of the dead boy's body, followed by my hours of traumatic dread capped off by the unwanted advances by Maria Dmitriyevna.

"Dear me," he mused, "this is all very troubling indeed." From his dispassionate tone, I could not discern whether he believed what I had just told him. Then again, if someone had narrated that same series of events to me, I would probably have difficulty believing him as well.

"What am I to do now?" I asked in hopes of receiving some wise counsel.

He looked up, he looked down, he looked away, and then he looked at me. "I think you need to go."

"Go? Where can I go?" His response was hardly the supportive guidance I had hoped for. "Is St. Petersburg even a possibility? They'll ask why I've returned. And it's so boring, Daniel Ivanovich. There's nothing for me to do there."

"Yes, well, it would be awkward, but you cannot remain here. You are not well at all." The concern I had grown to love from this man had returned to his voice.

"What am I to do now?" I repeated blankly. A painted Greek drum on the table caught my attention.

"After all, I have no idea what terms you worked out with the Sorokins, and whether you owe them or they owe you any money. Without money, it would be impossible to travel. How far would you be able to go?"

"What am I to do now?" How pitiful I had become.

He coughed and cleared his dry throat. "If you trust my temperament, and if you did not invent those God-knows-what stories, then I propose that you travel with me, Smurov." His face gave no clues as to his reason for this brilliant invitation.

"Where would we go?"

"Beyond the borders of our beloved Russia." The beaming smile returned to his spritely face.

"But I have no money, Daniel Ivanovich."

"We'll get by. Then, after a while, we can settle up. Once we've reached Rome we will be able to determine with whom you could return and where I'll go next. That might be for the best, I believe."

"Are you serious, Daniel Ivanovich? You wouldn't mind me travelling with you?"

"Why would I not be serious, Vanya?"

"Is that really possible? Me? In Rome?"

"Very much so," smiled my Greek teacher.

"I cannot believe it!" The excitement grew within me. From the point of total despair to the height of enthusiasm. I had travelled very far in a short period of time with no money at all.

"So... tomorrow morning I will speak with your Auntie Anna and let her know of our plans."

Once again I had to take the only option available to me, but this time I have been presented with the most wonderful opportunity! I will travel outside of my homeland for the very first time and get to see the ancient marvels that helped build our modern civilisation.

We stayed awake all through the night, discussing the trip, proposed stops, cities, and towns. Just as we were making our plans for sightseeing, the sun came up. I went to the window and pulled back the curtain and saw the daybreak, bright on the lane overgrown with opalescent grass. I couldn't believe I was still in Vasilsursk looking at the Volga and the dark woods beyond.

Part Three
Vanya says, Go! (Уезжайте)

*T*HIS!... THIS IS ROME!

What a contrast from the train ride into St. Petersburg earlier in the year. As we pulled into Rome, the tracks pass a double-arch entry portal, and I could see some of the ancient history of the beautiful city as we approached the terminal. So much better than that fairly-new St. Petersburg, with its grey squatness and boring squalor. Even the smells of Rome seemed fresh and exotic.

My first rail voyage came soon after the death of my mother, and I had travelled with a relative I hardly knew. Tears of sadness and grief blinded me, and I had allowed myself to be subjected to torment by the irresponsible and bourgeois Kazanskys. I later realised that is was people just like them who stirred up the masses to call for social upheaval.

This time, I was journeying with my dear Greek teacher, Daniel Ivanovich, a man I have come to know and respect. Instead of a train ride toward despair and uncertainty, this passage brought immeasurable delight as an expedition of exploration and discovery into glorious Rome.

We took a room in Vicolo del Lupo, an alleyway near Via del Corso. The window opened into the alley, and all we could see was the building across. It didn't matter because we spent very little time in the very little room.

Daniel Ivanovich paraded me around the City, taking me to galleries and museums during the day, and to the opera house in the evening. One night it was *The Barber of Seville* at Teatro Argentina, and the next it was *Il Trovatore* at Teatro Apollo.

A friend of Daniel Ivanovich, Hugo Orsini, accompanied us on most of our adventures. Orisini seemed to be sweating constantly, frequently swabbing his clean-shaven, plump, round face with a lace handkerchief. Although his dark eyes had no lustre, they communicated a sense of joy and wonder. His lips formed a permanent twist, and they matched in colour the ever-present carnation of his jacket buttonhole.

One evening, after we had attended *Tannhäuser* at Teatro dell'Opera, we sat in a caffè along Via del Corso, not far from our room. Around me I could hear the noisy, friendly Italian dialect, the clinking of plates, glasses with ice, and the remote scolding sound of a string orchestra through the veil of tobacco smoke. I felt myself almost intimate, feeling especially sociable and inclined to be close and yet separate.

At the next table sat a military officer with an entire cock's wings on his hat, and two ladies in flashy black dresses. I tried not to pay attention to them, and through the tulle hanging in the open window I could see the street lights, the passing carriages, passers-by on the sidewalk and on the roadway, even the nearest fountain on the piazza across from us.

I must have appeared quite boyish in my own traditional Russian outfit. It seemed somehow foppish in Rome, despite being fairly common dress at home. It made me appear very pale, tall and thin. Daniel Ivanovich, as he liked to joke, referred to himself as the "Chaperone of the Travelling Prince."

Orsini set down his espresso, wiped his forehead and launched into this evening's discourse. "Whenever I hear the first act of the second version–the Paris version where Wagner has Tristan and Isolde already onstage–I feel an unprecedented excitement, the thrill of the prophetic, as in the paintings of Klinger and the poetry of D'Annunzio. Dancing fauns and nymphs suddenly revealed, glowing, radiant, unprecedented imagination, but profoundly painful in familiar ancient landscapes. The apparition of Leda and Europa; cupids shooting from the trees, as in Botticelli's 'Spring.' Prancing fauns made motionless by painful arrows, adopting arduous poses, and all this before Venus, the guardian, with unearthly love and affection for the sleeping Tannhäuser. And then the wafting of a new spring, novel, boiling from the darkest depths of passion for life and for the sun!" He wiped his perspiration-moistened face with the lace again.

"It's the only time that Wagner refers to the ancients," added Daniel Ivanovich, "and I have seen this opera more than once–but not including the prelude scene with Venus–and I had always thought that she was synonymous with 'Parsifal' and Wagner's greatest concepts; however, I do not understand nor do I accept their conclusions. What is this renunciation? Asceticism? Neither of the characters, nor the genius of Wagner, nothing draws me to such conclusions!"

"Yes, well," Orsini began, "I grant you, the music does not particularly fit with what he had previously written, and Venus is an anæmic version of Isolde."

"As you are a musician, *Signor* Orsini, you would know more than me, and I respect your beliefs, but isn't this more the realm of poetry and philosophy?"

"Asceticism is, in fact, the most unnatural of phenomena, and the chastity of some animals is pure fancy." Orsini raised his handkerchief with a flourish.

While this Hugo Orsini certainly orated as well as anyone I had encountered in Russia, at least I understood most of his references. My Greek teacher had instructed me well on the ways of legend and opera, and he also made sure I understood the mythological histories with some depth. However, something about Orsini's character, perhaps the way he held himself, or maybe the flower in his shiny lapel, raised indefinite feelings of mistrust within me.

A waiter placed three servings of ice cream and water in large glasses with tall stems. I picked up the long-handled spoon and dipped it into the frozen dessert. The sour lemon flavour was so strong I could only take small bits without puckering, followed by mouthfuls of water. So much time had passed since we first sat down that most people had left the caffè, and the musicians had to play their repertoire a second time.

"You're leaving tomorrow?" Hugo asked me as he readjusted the carnation buttonhole.

"No, sir. I would like to depart from Rome, but not from Daniel Ivanovich. I'd like to travel with him for a bit longer, but he won't let me."

"And so, Daniel, you are off to Naples and Sicily. What about the boy?"

"I am sending him to Florence to spend some time with the Monsignor."

Orsini raised his eyebrows in surprise. "Mori?"

"Exactly."

"How do you know him, Daniel?"

"We met at Gaetano Bossi's, you know, the archaeologist."

"The one who lives in Via Nazionale?"

"Yes," Daniel Ivanovich smiled. "He is very sweet, this Monsignor," and he raised and lowered his eyebrows quickly.

Orsini laughed and addressed me, "Yes, and now I can truly say *nunc dimittis*, you are dismissed... from my own hands into those of the Monsignor."

I laughed quietly and asked playfully, "Really? Am I that annoying to you, Daniel Ivanovich?"

"Frightfully!" he spat, and we all laughed.

"We could all meet up in Florence," Orsini suggested. "I'll be there week next, and they will be playing my quartet."

"I am glad to hear of that. You know, you can always find the Monsignor at the cathedral, and he will certainly have my address."

"And I shall be lodging with the Marquise Moratti, in the village of Santi Apostoli. Please don't stand on ceremony. The Marquise lives alone and loves to meet new people. She is my aunt, and I am her successor." He smiled sweetly with his delicate mouth, and his round, white face with the lustreless black eyes. His rings sparkled on his well-developed musical fingers with their short-cropped fingernails.

Perhaps it was his eyes that distressed me. And it didn't help to know he was the nephew and heir of a marquise. As Daniel

Ivanovich and I walked back to our room, I said, "That Hugo Orsini seems a bit noxious, doesn't he?"

The Greek teacher looked at me with a quizzical expression. "What kind of made-up twaddle is that? Hugo is a very nice man, nothing more." He frowned. "It worries me, Vanya, that you are so quick to see the worst in others. Perhaps if you looked only at their best qualities instead we would all be better off, especially you."

~ Π ~

Despite the light rain streaming in rivulets along the pavement down the hill, the coolness inside the museum felt pleasant and desirable in contrast. After spending Daniel Ivanovich's last day in Rome visiting the Colosseum, the Forum, and the Palatine Hill, our final stop was this particular gallery he wanted me to experience. We stood, nearly alone, in a small room before two sculpted figures of "running boys."

"Only the torso, the so-called 'Ilium,' can be compared with the life and beauty of the youthful body, which can be seen below the white skin, like flowing crimson blood, where all the muscles are intoxicating, captivating, and where we, as contemporaries, are not hampered by a lack of hands and head." Daniel Ivanovich acted as docent and philosopher. "The body itself, its substance, will perish, and works of art, Phidias, Mozart, Shakespeare, for example, will die. However, the idea, the kind of beauty enclosed in them, cannot be lost, and it may be the only value in a changing and transient diversity of life. And no matter how coarse or crude the implementation of these ideas, they are divine and pure. Religious practises, perhaps, are an exception because they do not take the form of the loftiest asceticism ideals in their symbolic rites. They may be wild and savage, but sanctified within them are hidden symbols. Is that at all divine?"

I might have not remembered parts of this particular rant of his as I was captivated by the forms of the naked young men captured in the midst of running. If only I could have met one of them and fallen in love. If only I looked like one of them, athletic and fetching.

Daniel Ivanovich clasped my shoulder, rousing me from the trance. "Smurov, listen to me," he instructed, "if you need spiritual consolation at a budget price, speak with the Monsignor, but if your money is all spent, or if you need wise and wonderful advice, contact Larion Dmitrievich. I'll give you his address. Yes? Promise me?"

"Really? Isn't there anyone else? I don't know if I want to bother with him again."

"I don't believe there is anyone more faithful to you than Stroop. However, if you would prefer someone else, go look for yourself." His clipped pronunciation suggested frustration with my determination.

"What? Hugo Orsini? He doesn't seem like he'd be much help."

"Hardly. He almost always has no money himself. I don't know what you have against Larion Dmitrievich. Even before, why wouldn't you write to him? What happened that could adequately explain this change in your heart?"

I just stared at the bust of Marcus Aurelius in his youth and did not answer immediately. It took a few minutes to assemble my reasoning, and finally I began slowly and monotonously, "I do not blame him, not in the least, I don't think I have the right to get angry, but I was unbearably sad to learn a few things, against my will. I cannot continue to discuss Stroop. It disturbs me to envision him as the sought-after mentor and friend."

"What romanticism!" Daniel Ivanovich clapped slowly, as if I had recited lines from Shakespeare. "However, it sounded as if learned by rote! You, like some of the other 'heavenly' ladies, imagine that gentlemen must be thinking that girls do not eat, do not drink, do not sleep, do not snore, do not blow their noses. Every person has their unorthodoxy. Not in the least does it humiliate them, no matter how disagreeable it might be in other people's eyes. And if you are jealous of Fyodor, it means you recognise yourself as his equal, that you have assigned yourself the same importance and purpose. But, oddly enough, it is far better than romantic insipidness."

"Let's drop this, please." He really touched on a sensitive subject I had no desire to discuss. "If it turns out there really is no other way, then I shall submit to calling upon Stroop."

"Well done, my little Cato." Now his condescendence became irritating, as he referred to me as the unpopular stoic Roman consul. What was it he withheld from me regarding Stroop that kept him pushing me in that direction?

"You, yourself, taught me to despise Cato."

"Apparently, I have not been particularly successful."

~ Π ~

After an uncomfortable night of tense silence between us, my Greek teacher, Daniel Ivanovich, who had been so good in allowing me to be his travelling companion at no cost, left quietly in the morning for Naples. Fortunately for me, he had paid in advance for the room and left me a ticket to Florence.

Later in the morning, Hugo Orsini called on me and asked if I would like to stroll through the grounds of Villa Borghese with him. Having nothing else to do, and almost no money to do it with, I grudgingly went along with Orsini. For one thing, it might have given me time to appreciate him a bit better and, perhaps, discover what Daniel Ivanovich found good in him. Secondly, it would probably have meant meals that I could not have otherwise paid for.

As we strolled along the giant maze of criss-crossing pathways, Orsini decided it would be jolly fun if he whistled his entire quartet to me. It sounded like a dreadful idea, but I had no choice but to feign interest. If the person paying for my meal wished to noodle the strains of his tiresome composition, then so be it. Besides, how could one man perform an entire quartet by himself?

From time to time, I caught Orsini looking at me in a way that reminded me all too much of Maria Dmitriyevna right before she attempted to take physical advantage. I decided to keep a comfortable distance between us.

By late afternoon we walked along a straight path through the lawn and flower beds with the indistinct colours of twilight toward the terrace. A delicate whitish mist crept, spilling behind us, attempting to catch up with us. Somewhere in the distance, a pack of owlets screamed. In the eastern sky, a shimmering star shone like a dancing feather through the pink mist. Directly opposite us, interlaced windows of the ancient residence lit up with an unusual and curious blaze, reflecting the kaleidoscopic sky off the glass.

Hugo mercifully tweeted the final notes of his composition and then silently smoked a cigarette as we continued on our way. As we passed through the garden terraces, toward the end of so many crossing paths, I heard two distinct Russian voices, a man and a woman. I stopped to listen. This might have been construed as eavesdropping, but I had not heard anyone speaking Russian in Rome up to that point, and my sense of curiosity overwhelmed my sense of propriety.

The man asked, "So, are you planning to stay a while in Italy?"

"I don't know. You see, my mother is weak. After Naples we'll stay in Lugano, and I don't know for how long."

"So long that I won't be able to see you," the man whined, "to hear your voice, to –"

"Only four months," hastily interrupted the woman.

"Four months!" the man echoed incredulously.

"I don't suppose that you would become bored..." she trailed off as we ascended the steps in twilight.

I could only make out the shadowy figure of a seated woman, and standing next to her a rather short man.

As we entered the transport station across the way, a crowded and sweltering room, I asked Hugo, "Who were those people speaking Russian?"

"Ummm..."–he struggled to recall–"...Blonskaya"–his eyes squinted as he thought–"Anna Blonskaya, and one of your artists." He waved a flabby hand, "I don't remember his name. Sergei, something-or-other, I believe."

"He seems to be quite taken with her."

"I think we all know that," he winked at me, "as well as his libertine lifestyle." He rolled his eyes.

"Is she beautiful?" I asked, realising too late how much more naïve it made me sound.

"Take a look for yourself." He pointed behind me.

When I turned round, I saw a thin, pale girl with smooth skin and delicate features enter the hall. Her dark hair brushed low over the ears, but I could still see her rather large mouth and vibrant blue eyes. A minute later, a man about ten years older than me quickly followed. He appeared hunched over, but I could see a pointy, blond beard and curly hair. His very pale eyes bulged beneath a set of bushy eyebrows the colour of old gold, and he had pointed ears, like a faun.

I turned back to Orsini and asked, "He loves her and leads a libertine life, and everyone knows it?"

"Well, he loves her too much–in my estimation–for fear that he might actually treat her like a woman. Russian whimsy!" The Italian pursed his lips.

As we walked toward the way out, I spied a rather stout clergyman, sweating profusely, rolling his eyes, and muttering, "His Holiness was so tired, so tired..."

Through the greyed window, a bright ray of light flashed abruptly, and the startled clergyman gazed heavenward, crossing himself vigorously. The muffled sound of carriage wheels grew louder.

"So, good-bye until Florence," Orsini said as he shook my hand, holding on just a little too long for my comfort.

I pulled my hand away with a jerk. "Yes, we shall dine again soon."

We went our separate ways and I still had to wonder what Daniel Ivanovich found so redeeming in this strange and self-centred man.

~ Π ~

The next morning, I went to the station and boarded the train to Florence. Orsini, and perhaps after a while Daniel Ivanovich, would be there, and at least I would know a few people. As lovely a city as Rome was, without friends it could be very lonely. All that sense of history, but those Romans were long dead.

The train through the Italian countryside provided some needed relief from time spent in a city. I could see farms, farmers, and farm animals. The Italian farms seemed much happier than the Russian farms I had known.

At the station in Florence, it didn't take very long to identify Monsignor Mori. Only one clergyman stood waiting and looking about. Even so, without his vestments, Mori was easy to identify. At 65 years of age, his stocky and ruddy frame hid within a flowing, black robe held with a plain rope belt.

We walked the few blocks to the monastery where I would be staying. Florence reminded me more of my own hometown, the few memories I had left. While it still held the mystique of its Roman past, the architecture tended to be more rustic than classical. The marketplace overflowed with vendors and shoppers.

"You do like to read, don't you?" Mori asked haltingly, as if he had never met or spoken with a Russian before.

"Yes. Yes, of course, my Greek teacher, whom I believe you know, Daniel Ivanovich, encourages me to absorb all I can."

"And I have heard that Mr. Stroop also tutors you in the English." The hint of a smile on the Monsignor's face suggested more than just a passing acquaintance. Is there anyone who has not met Larion Dmitriyevich?

"Yes. He gifted me a volume of Shakespeare, and I read it–well, as much of it as I could understand, that is."

"Good. Good," he chanted as he waddled along. "On my library shelves you will find texts in Italian, Latin, French, Spanish, English and Greek. Aquinas next to Don Quixote, your very Shakespeare mixed in with the disparate lives of saints, Seneca cosying up to Anacreon."

"Anacreon?" I had thought his hedonistic writing had been banned by the Roman Catholics.

"Oh, yes. I confiscated the book from one of my spiritual children," he explained. He must have seen the surprised look on my face because he went on to justify himself, "I have many confiscated books in my library. You see, to me, they cannot bring harm." He smiled contently.

We turned into a dark, narrow street. The shadows cooled the air. At the far end we stopped in front of a heavy wooden door. Instead of a knocker, a single wrought iron ring hung adorning the portal. Monsignor Mori pushed on the ring and the door swung open. There appeared to be no lock and no latch.

As we went into the entry hall, I could hear women's voices off to one side. Through an archway I could see half a dozen nuns lounging upon colourful, embroidered pillows in the window-sills of a courtyard. When they saw us enter, they burst up upon us, shrieking and yelping.

"Ulysses," one of them bleated, "you said you were going to retrieve the Russian *signor* who will live with us."

"This is my sister, Poldina," Mori informed me blandly, as if she were no more than a passer-by.

"Ulysses, I thought you were joking. No one has ever lived with us before. And now you bring this prince, this Russian noble-man. How are we to look after such a fine person?"

Mori started to move down the hall. "This way, Vanya."

I followed him, but Poldina continued to prattle on, "But don't you worry, my brother, we will make do." She seemed to be sizing me up. "We had thought a Russian *signor* would be large, stout and tall. However, you have delivered to us a little boy, so thin, so dear, a cherub," the old woman's voice sof-tened tenderly in sweet cadences.

The monsignor tucked his robe and climbed a narrow set of circular stone stairs. His thick calves bulged in their black, home-knitted stockings funnelled into thick shoes. Because of his age and size, he moved rather slowly and with much pant-ing. I followed him to a large, open chamber. "This is my library," he announced with pride. He walked to one of the many desks and pointed. "These are the theological doctrine tracts I would like you to examine because, in my view, I be-lieve you will find them most interesting."

We walked through and into another corridor. A few doors past, he turned and we entered a small apartment. "Here is your room."

I had expected the accommodations at a monastery to be minimal and ascetic, like my previous lodgings, but this room seemed about the same size as the Kazansky dining hall. Framed drawings of saints covered the walls, blue and white curtains hung in the window next to a Madonna of Good Counsel, and in the midst of it all, a canopy bed. Below the window stood a small table and next to it a shelf with educational books. Beside the bookshelf stood a small dresser with a painted, wax figurine of St. Luigi Gonzaga dressed in a suit made from scraps of altar boys' robes. To keep it clean, a dusty bell jar covered it. When I looked back at the door, attached to the inside frame was a vessel of holy water. If it weren't for the grand size of the room, it felt something like what I would have imagined a monk's cell might have been like. I turned toward the door to the balcony and saw a dressing table next to an old upright piano. Surely such luxury comes at a price, but that amount had not yet been discussed.

Mori's sister, Poldina, rushed by, "Cat! Ah! Cat! Shoo! Shoo!"

A large, fluffy white tomcat appeared briefly seeming somewhat triumphant after running up the wooden staircase from the entry hall below.

"Oh, please don't chase it off on my account." I thought back to the crippled kitten that Daniel Ivanovich had taken in. "I love cats."

"The *signor* loves cats!" Poldina cooed, her face wrinkling up into deep crevices. "Oh, my son! Oh, my dear!" She faced the stairwell and yelled, "Philumena, bring Miscina and her kittens to show the *signor*..." She turned to Mori. "Such a dear..."

~ Π ~

The next morning, we walked about Florence, and the Monsignor's melodious and loud voice reported information, events, and anecdotes from the 14th and our dawning 20th Centuries equally–with enthusiasm and interest–relating the scandalous chronicle of our own time in contrast to the story of a former resident of Florence, the painter Vasari. He stopped in the middle of crowded alleyways in order to elaborate on their eloquent and, for the most part, incriminating periods. Mori seemed to speak to everyone–passers-by, horses, dogs–with his loud laughing and singing, creating his own atmosphere around him. He spoke rather politely, like a commoner, but with a rude delicacy, uncomplicated yet informative, all with his own peculiar gaiety. It reminded me of the ambiance in some of Sacchetti's short stories.

Sometimes, when the supply of tales did not satisfy his need to talk, so to speak, with his dramatic intonation and gestures, he would start a conversation about a primitive work of art, and then he returned to the old subject–novelists–and discussed them again with a naïve eloquence and conviction. He knew everyone and everything. Every corner stone of his Tuscany and sweet Florence had its legends and anecdotal historicity.

He led me everywhere, taking advantage of his position as a human traveller. There were worn-out marquises and counts living in neglected palaces playing cards and quarrelling about it with their footmen. There were engineers, doctors, and merchants living simply, like in the old days: economically and closed off from others. I saw young musicians aspiring to Puccini's fame, attempting to imitate him with their fancy silk cravats and thick, beardless faces. I met the Persian consul, an important and supportive man who lived out near San Miniato, and his six fat nieces. There was a chemist and a few errand boys with parcels. Monsignor Mori introduced me to a few Englishwomen who had converted to Catholicism and, finally, Mme. Monier.

A French émigrée, she was an æsthete and artist who lived in Fiesole, just north of the city, entertaining a whole company of guests in her villa painted with soft spring allegories overlooking Florence and the Arno valley. She seemed well-suited to the Monsignor: always cheerful, somewhat tall, constantly prattling, ginger-coloured, and fairly unattractive.

We stayed on the front terrace at a table with a pinkish tablecloth into the evening. The heavily murky sky, already muddy with an impending dusk, appeared entirely dark red, like a puddle of blood. I could hear the clinking of plates mixed with the smell of cigar smoke, wine in unfinished glasses, and strawberries mingled with the floral scent from the garden. From the house a woman's voice sang old songs, interrupted by brief silences. Around me, prolonged talking and laughter occasionally caught my ears. When the fire was set alight inside, the view from the terrace took on a dimly-lit setting, resembling the staging for Maeterlinck's poetic drama, *L'Interieur.*

Hugo Orsini, pale and beardless, with the ever-present carnation buttonhole, spoke with a few others on the terrace. He went on to say, "You cannot imagine how he loses himself in a woman. If the person is not an ascetic, there is no greater crime than pure love. Being in love with Blonskaya, he can only see what is at her level. Well, with this new woman–and I almost hesitate to call her that–Cibo, it is only her depraved mermaid eyes in a pale face. Her mouth, oh, her mouth! Just listen to the things she says. There is no expletive that she had not repeated, and her every word: vulgarity! She is the girl in that fairy tale who, each time she tried to speak, a mouse or a toad jumped out of her mouth. Positively! And she will not let go. Because of her, he forgets about Blonskaya, his talent, and everything for this woman. She has killed a man, specifically, an artist."

No one responded to his accusation, but it made me curious. "And do you think that if Blonskaya... if he loved her at all, he could break off with Cibo?"

Orsini turned his head toward me, as if it surprised him that anyone would ask such a question. "I think he would, yes."

I still did not fully understand the mechanics of grown-up love, and I recklessly continued, "Do you think him incapable of chaste love?"

"Can't you see what will happen? You will need to look at his face in order to understand it. I would never claim to know because you cannot be sure of anything, but I can see that he is perishing. I see why, and it infuriates me because I love him so very much and appreciate his works. I equally hate Cibo and Blonskaya." Orsini finished smoking his cigarette, tamped it on the sole of his shoe and went into the house.

I sat there alone, thinking about the stoop-shouldered artist with blond, curly hair and a pointed beard, bright grey eyes under thick, arched eyebrows the colour of old gold, mocking and sad. And then, for some reason, I thought about Stroop.

From the hall came the voice of Mme. Monier, like a melodramatic bird, "Remember that genius Segantini's painting with vast wings above the lovers near a spring on the heights? All lovers should have wings like that, so they can be daring, free, and affectionate."

"Yes, well"–I could hear Orsini clear his throat–"I just received word from my connection in Paris that Anatole France himself has given his blessing and nod to my composition. I kiss your very name"–and a loud pucker sound resonated out onto the terrace–"O, great teacher!"

"Your composition? The one based on D'Annunzio's poetry? Of course, of course! Why have you been so silent?" The scraping noise of moving chairs flooded the room, and then the piano, with loud, proud chords. After a few opening measures, the voice of Orsini followed on a somewhat banal melody with a silly, broad passion.

"Oh, I'm so glad to hear that! Which fellow did you say? Wonderful!" chirped Mme. Monier. She ran out onto the terrace, dressed all in pink, contrasting her ginger-red features, hideous and charming. "Ah! You're still here!" she chimed upon seeing me sitting like a Rodin sculpture. "I have some good news for you! Your compatriot has arrived. But he is not a Russian, although he is from St. Petersburg, I believe. He has always been a great friend to me. Is he an Englishman? Eh? What?" she tossed out her questions. Without waiting for an answer, then she dashed off to meet the arriving visitors on the wide carriageway in the garden. The moon had already risen, and it enveloped the town with its pale radiance.

Stroop?! Here in Florence? How could that be? I did not want to stay and hear the answers to those questions. "For goodness sake!" I sputtered unintentionally. "Can't you just leave me alone," I whispered to myself although the words were more for Stroop. "Mori! Mori!" I cried out, and rushed to the Monsignor sitting inside. "I am afraid I cannot deal with this right now. Can we leave without saying our good-byes? Please? Now. This instant!"

Mori held a large glass of ice cream in one hand and a spoon in the other. His eyes bulged out at my impertinence. His brows knitted in thought and then, at once, his expression softened. "Well, yes. Certainly, my child, but I do not understand what worries you so. Come on, I just need to find my hat." He set the glass and spoon on the table and moved slowly to the hat rack.

"Hurry! Hurry, *cher père*!" Terror coursed through my blood, and we could not move fast enough. "This way! This way!" I latched onto the arm of the Monsignor, pulling him out of the house. "They're right there!" I tugged him off to the side of the main road, as a carriage passed by. The sound of hooves and carriage wheels nearly deafened me. Then at the curve of the narrow path, bathed in moonlight, unexpectedly close to us, we met Mme. Monier and a few guests who had taken a shortcut. Everyone stopped where they stood.

And there, unmistakable in the clear light, without a doubt: Stroop.

"Let's stay," I whispered, squeezing the Monsignor's arm. My eyes were focused on Larion Dmitriyevich, handsome as ever, but I could feel Mori's gaze shining down upon my flushed, beaming face. He must have been thinking how much trouble this new pupil might pose, no matter how angelic I might have looked in the innocent moonlight.

Everyone funnelled into the fire-lit parlour, and I sat off to the side, out of the way, as far from Stroop as I could. Bottles of chianti appeared and Mme. Monier's staff went around filling everyone's glass with the blood-like wine.

The others discussed and argued, opined and pointed fingers until the orange light of dawn matched the orange light of the glowing embers in the fireplace. Instead of speaking directly with him, I utilised my time observing Larion Dmitriyevich, watching his postures, scrutinising his language, listening and watching for clues to his true nature. As it seems that fate keeps finding ways to put us together, I wanted to make certain that he genuinely was a good man, and a good man for me.

~ Π ~

Later in the morning, Mme. Monier decided we would all ride up to the mountain ridge where one could see both the Mediterranean and the Adriatic Seas. "There's no place like it in the entire world!" She chirped. "It's spectacular!"

Stroop announced he needed to go back to Florence to conduct some business. I had thoughts of asking him if I might accompany him but then decided it might be best to leave him conduct his business on his own. He had said he planned to spend a few days in the area before heading off to his next destination, and I was sure we would get to converse some more later.

The parties divided up into four donkey carts, and we rumbled up the Tuscan countryside, passing vineyards and farms among the paths lined with chestnut trees. Others complained of the uncomfortable ride, but I already had some experience in such rustic vehicles. Soon we began to see birch, pine, moss, and violets, and it seemed the clouds were just out of reach. After a while, the roads switched back and forth until we finally attained the summit of Giugnola. To the east, I could see the town of Faenza, and to the south, the spectacular Firenzuola, looking like a handful of red and gray stones piled on top of each other. Some of the people looked this way and that, observing both bodies of water, barely visible on the distant horizons.

While we stood enjoying the views, an old-fashioned stage-coach coming the other way pulled off the road to give one of the women passengers a chance to deal with one of nature's urgencies.

A few members of the party suggested we get back down the mountain before nightfall. Mme. Monier grudgingly agreed, and we piled into the carts again and started back down the way we had come.

We stopped at a ruined villa just outside of San Lorenzo. An informational sign posted on the gate stated that the original house was built in the 13th Century. The centre of the fortress was large enough for a shepherd's hut, and there was an old well off to the side, which would have come in handy during sieges. The dining hall was on the level above, and on the way to the stairwell at the rear, we walked past the library and the chapel. Portraits of nobles hung on every wall. Knowing that the structure was around 700 years old, I expected the staircase to be thin and splintery. However, it must have been replaced some time in the last 100 years because the tread steps seemed thick and sturdy.

We sat at the one remaining free table, and soon the tanned, curvy hostess with long raven hair brought cold plates of scrambled eggs, cheese, and salami, with chianti and coffee to drink. All talking ceased. The only sounds were of forks and knives on plates, and spoons in cups.

A few diners ate at the two other tables and the hostess sat off to the side next to a big-eyed man with black brows, no jacket, and a green trilby hat. When people began smoking, it seemed more like a thieves' den than a tavern.

It was no surprise when Mme. Monier spoke up. "How this reminds me of one of blessed Goldoni's works! What delightful simplicity!" She clapped her red-handled parasol on the table.

The man with the green hat leaned back in his wooden chair as the hostess reported, "I told the gentleman: It has long been known that my Beppo is here at night... Then the Carabinieri said to me: 'Auntie Pasca, do not disdain our money, but Beppo will still be caught.' I thought they wouldn't dare. I'm an honest woman, look... But fate will always be fate. And there was the time he came to his countryman's wedding drunk and went to bed... 'Pasca, we warned you earlier,' the Carabinieri whistled. They had taken knives and guns from Beppo before. What could he do?" She wagged her head side to side.

The man stared to say, "Woman..."

"How he swore!" she interrupted. "Even though he was all tied up, he kicked at the legs of the bench he was sitting on. It collapsed, and he began to roll around on the floor!" Pasca roared in a hoarse voice, smiling with gleaming teeth, as if telling the most pleasant thing. She winked at the fellow listening.

"Yes, well, you are one fine woman," he responded.

"Pasca, can I get a refill?" A bearded man at another table held up a ceramic goblet.

The hostess stood and approached him. "Another one?" she asked while reaching for the man's hand.

"You are well-shaped," he offered, clapping the hostess on the rump as she took away the empty cup.

The woman turned back with a flushed and angry look on her face. She pointed a wagging finger at the patron, "Hey! You keep your hands where they belong, *signor*, or my Beppo might call on you some evening to remove them!"

~ Π ~

Getting back out into the bright clean air felt good after spending an hour or so in the smoky tavern. Just as I was about to hop up into one of the donkey carts, Mme. Monier cried out, "*Signor* Orsini, I seemed to have left my parasol on the table. Could you retrieve it for me, please? We shall wait for you!" The donkeys brayed loudly at her squealing. She held out a pale, dainty hand, and Mori assisted her into the first carriage.

We waited for Hugo to return, beholding the beauty of the hillside. After a few minutes, Mme. Monier stood, and the cart wobbled unsteadily. Once she got her bearings, she squawked, "*Signor* Smurov, please go see what is keeping *Signor* Orsini."

Her instruction caught me unawares, and I did not respond straightaway. Someone in the party cleared their throat. I then realised she had addressed me directly, and I turned to her, "I am sorry. What did you say, Mme. Monier?"

"Eh? what? My parasol, my parasol!" and she waved her hand at me as if I were one of her servants. I had horrible thoughts of retrieving the cursed thing and then depositing it where there would be no *sol* to *para*. Before sitting in the wagon again, she began arranging her ugly pink dress and her flowing red tresses with a silly, smiling face.

When I got back up to the tavern, no one was about. All the plates and cups still remained on the tables. Only the shifted positions of the benches and chairs indicated there had been former patrons. In one of the arches hung a dark curtain, and I could hear sighs and vague whispers from behind it.

"Who's there?" I called out.

"What do you want?" a raspy woman's voice responded.

"One of our party left her parasol. Have you seen it?"

More whispering could be heard from behind the curtain. Then Pasca, the hostess, appeared, looking rather dishevelled without her shawl or bodice. Her previously smooth, dark hair, had come undone. She tugged nervously at her dirty skirt as she took a few steps toward me.

I could see that her voluptuous, tanned, body might appeal to some other men. She stared at me for a second as if sizing me up for some sort of business transaction, then she nodded and pointed to the corner. There stood the faded, old parasol. It had white lace trim with an indefinite yellowish pattern on top and a red handle. I picked it up and started walking back toward the stairs.

From behind the curtain, a male voice whispered, "Pasca? Pasca? Are you coming back soon? Have they gone?"

"Just now," she said hoarsely. As I started out, I turned back and saw her looking into the fragment of a mirror on the wall as she slipped into her mussed-up hair a carnation the colour of Orsini's lips.

~ Π ~

When we returned to the monastery, I went to my room straightaway. The day's events had exhausted me, and I needed to rest.

As I lay down on the large, reasonably comfortable canopy bed, I began to wonder why I had been given such luxurious accommodations. My fear had been that I would have to provide something in return, such as physical labour, or perhaps giving language lessons, but no one had instructed me to do anything but read and study the texts left by the Monsignor.

I heard light footsteps outside the room. My curiosity had kept me from falling asleep, and I went to the door and opened it. There stood Sister Poldina holding some linens. She smiled up at me with her weathered face.

"Is everything to your liking, *signor*?"

"Yes, thank you, sister." She peered into the room behind me. "Is there something you wish, sister?"

"I have fresh bedclothes. May I?" Her eyes bulged in the direction of the bed.

"Sister, I have hardly slept here since my arrival. I don't think there is any need to replace the linens I have hardly used." At home we would keep the same sheets for months at a time. At the Kazansky house, the servants changed the beds of the family with some frequency, but the one I slept in seemed to have the same linens day after day.

"Of course, *signor*, if you would prefer..." she turned away with a sulking look.

"Sister," I called out before she reached the top of the stairs, "may I ask you something?" I thought that perhaps she could help explain the mystery of my room assignment.

"Yes!" she brightened up immediately. "Anything, *signor*. Anything at all."

"Well... sister...," I wasn't quite sure how to phrase the question. Her bright, stonewashed eyes stared up at me as if the next word might be modern gospel. "I was wondering why I have been blessed with such a... spacious room, and I have not been required to assist with the housework."

Poldina smiled from ear to flappy ear. Her hands grasped the linens as if they were the beloved Shroud of Turin. "Oh, *signor*. I know you prefer not to speak of such things, but Hugo Orsini mentioned to the Monsignor that you are a Travelling Prince. We could not have the Russian royalty performing such menial tasks. Your duties are only to absorb the teachings of the Monsignor and the texts he provides to you." She bowed slightly, as if I were actually noble before she trundled her way down the narrow stairs.

Russian royalty? Travelling Prince? Where did these ludicrous ideas come from? It took a few moments to recall that Daniel Ivanovich liked to refer to himself as the "Chaperone of the Travelling Prince." My ordinary Russian peasant attire–bold-coloured shirts with stiff collars and embroidered trim–blended in with everyone else at home. Here in Italy, people wore more muted tones, and I sort of stood out.

I realised I had a bit of a dilemma before me: Should I keep silent and continue to enjoy the privileges afforded to me because of the misunderstanding, or should I confess the truth about being nothing more than a mere orphan wanting a home?

The more I thought about it, the more I realised there was no need to rush to any conclusion. Being mistaken for a Russian prince was not the worst thing that could happen to a young man in my situation. Once I had resolved the issue in my mind, I lay back on the featherbed and drifted off into a restful sleep.

~ Π ~

The following evening Stroop, Orsini, and I attended the opera at Teatro Goldoni in Florence. Obtaining a box did not seem to be of any difficulty because the house seemed fairly empty. It was to be another work of Wagner, this time *Tristan und Isolde*. I found the German works quite pompous and excessively allegorical. The Italian scores were playful and mischievous, much more to my liking.

As it turned out, I sat between the two men. Orsini, who fashioned himself as a composer and *bon vivant*, lived his life as if the orchestra was playing underscore music to accompany his every stylised, artistic action. Stroop, on the other hand, was serious-minded, handsome and mysterious, like the leading gent of many operatic works.

Just as Isolde began "*Befehlen ließ dem Eigenholde*," requesting her maid, Brangäne, to fetch Tristan for her, a crowd of people trampled into the hall. At the front of the pack stood a bored-looking and business-like little man with an unwaxed moustache. His head seemed too large for his frame, and his face appeared sentimental but toughened.

I must have clucked my tongue without thinking because Stroop leaned over and whispered in my ear, "Young man, that is King Emmanuel. Show some respect."

Respect? Even though he might be the King of Italy, he and his entourage had interrupted the performance with their leisurely entrance. The house lights had come up, and ladies in nearby boxes strained their backs leaning over the railing just to get a glimpse of their ruler. Shiny necklaces and décolletage hung from their low-cut gowns, and it made me giggle to see them labouring so.

King Emmanuel bowed to the audience, and the people cheered and applauded loudly. He proceeded to the royal box off to the side of the stage, and sat at the rail, still looking rather world-weary. The houselights dimmed, and the onstage action resumed.

At the interval, people milled about in their boxes. The well-dressed ladies chatted with the well-dressed gentlemen, who looked cavalier with their fancy buttonholes. Some people even visited from box to box, exchanging words and smiles. It all seemed so polite but tedious.

Servers came through with ice cream. Some of the older men sat at the rear of their boxes reading newspapers.

Even though I happened to be situated between Orsini and Stroop, I heard not a whisper nor sound around me as my mind had been totally absorbed with the thoughts of Isolde as she stood staring into a brazier, listening to the hunting horns with her maid, Brangäne. Instead of the requested potion of atonement for the forbidden love between Tristan and Isolde, the maid had prepared a love potion. All Isolde needed to do was extinguish the flame, and Tristan would directly appear before her to plead his troth. Did I see myself in Isolde the way I had previously identified with Micaëla, the lovelorn maiden in *Carmen*? Had I taken the love draught unknowingly? Where was the fire I must quench in order to signal unending devotion to my lover?

"This is the apotheosis of love!" Hugo broke into my meditation with one of his sentimental declarations. "Even without the realm of the night and someone worth dying for, it would still be a great song of passion. The shape of the melody itself, and the whole scene is like a ritual, like an anthem or a hymn!"

For some reason I did not understand, I went completely ashen upon hearing his litany.

Stroop stared through his opera glasses at the box across from us. I followed his gaze and saw the blond artist, Sergei–I think that's what Orsini called him–sitting very close to a small woman with bright black wavy hair. Her unnatural pale eyes seemed so huge in her whitish face with no rouge. In contrast, her thick lips glowed from so much red paint. The woman and her bright-yellow dress embroidered with gold both stood out. She held her vulgar chin pretentiously and looked simply demonic.

I had heard various stories about the adventures of this Veronica Cibo. Most were accusations entwined with different names of men and women who lost their lives because of her.

"There she is, the wench!" spat Hugo upon espying her. "Her type belongs back in the 16th Century." But he still kept staring at her as if she were a carnival attraction.

"Oh, Hugo," Stroop contributed, "you're being far too easy on her. It is simple: she is a despicable witch. Some of the coarsest names you will ever hear have escaped from the lips of proper gentlemen who have gazed with desire upon that yellow dress and the lecherous, mermaid blue eyes sunken into her pallid face."

I really wanted to ask Stroop about her, but I just sat there blushing and smiling, like we had recently made up from a violent quarrel or one of us had recovered from a long illness.

Hugo stood and went out into the corridor, and I followed him.

"It makes me think of Tristan and Isolde," I said once we left the box. "It is the depiction of perfect love, the apotheosis of passion, as you have said. However, I mean, if you look at it from the outside, and the end of the story, is it not the same situation we found at the tavern in San Lorenzo?"

"I don't quite understand what you mean." His already pale face blanched even further, and he shifted his weight from foot to foot as if uncomfortable with the topic. "Are you embarrassed about the portrayal of carnal interaction on the stage?"

"No, not at all. At least *that* is a real act of humour and humiliation. Well, after all, Isolde and Tristan needed to undress onstage, and they took off their clothing. Don't you find their slickers and trousers just as unappealing as the jackets we are both wearing?" I pointed a finger at me and then him.

"Oh! Such thoughts!" Orsini began laughing. "How funny you are, Vanya." He seemed surprised by my question.

"You know," I responded, "it seems to me that this has frequently been the case. Sometimes I have no idea what you're talking about." That might have been a bit cruel, but it certainly was spot on. "Just the bare essence, please. Isn't it all the same? Does it really matter how we arrive at the act? Whether it is the expression of love or just an animalistic outburst?"

"What is wrong with you? What has Monsignor Mori done to you?" His face began to regain some of the lost colouring. "Of course, the facts and bare essence–as you put it–are not important, but it is crucial that we treat them as if they were. Even the most outrageous fact, or the most far-fetched position, can be proven and purified in relation to itself," Orsini said quite seriously, almost like a school lecture.

I smiled and replied, "Maybe that's true, in spite of your condemnation!" I opened the door to our box, went in and sat down next to Stroop. Looking at him from the side, I had a much different view of the man from before. Could he be my Don José? My Tannhäuser? My Tristan?

The three of us watched the final act without saying a word to each other. Tristan returned, battle-scarred and bandaged. He died in Isolde's arms, muttering her name. The maid, Brangäne, confessed giving them a potion for love instead of atonement. Isolde belted out "*Liebestod*" to a rousing ovation, and then she died too.

Love and Death. Love and Death. So divinely connected, as if one surely led to the other.

~ Π ~

At a too early hour the next morning, our little entourage went to see Mme. Monier off at the station for her voyage to Brittany, where she planned to spend a week or two before heading on to Paris.

The sky hadn't become quite blue yet, and the small electric globes glared white against the pale yellow sky, crying, PRONTI – PARTENZA. We sat in the concourse, and I watched people bustle about. Some seemed to be waiting for the same train to France, and others seemed like passengers from an earlier train. From the refreshment room I could hear constant requests and tinkling spoons.

We sat drinking coffee while waiting for Mme. Monier's train. On the table lay a bouquet of *Gloire de Dijon* roses atop an opened *Figaro* next to the lady's gloves. For her travels, Mme. Monier wore a maize-coloured dress with pale yellow ribbons.

Orsini made some remarks he thought witty regarding recent political news. I didn't pay much attention to him as I did not care for any discussion of current events, and even less for anything said by Hugo Orisini.

Veronica Cibo sat down at a neighbouring table in dark red travelling clothes with a bright green veil covering her hideous face. The hunched artist, Sergei, sat next to her, clutching a portmanteau, and behind them, a porter held other belongings.

"Well, look at that!" Orsini cried out, "They are also taking the train to France." He stood and walked to greet the hapless artist.

I turned to look at Stroop, who sat sipping an Italian coffee. Even at dawn he presents an intriguing silhouette. If only there were some topic I could conjure up to discuss. I found the more I spoke with him, the more I wanted to spend time engaging him.

He turned and caught me gawking at him. A smile appeared on his striking face and he asked, "Is there something you wish to discuss, Vanya?"

Again, I was dumbstruck and could not speak. He took another sip from the demitasse. My head dropped, heavy from such thoughts, and then I realised I wanted to ask him how long he planned to stay in Florence and where his next destination might be. However, before I could take a breath, a loud gasp nearby derailed my action.

"And where do they think *they're* going?" Mme. Monier chirped. "Is he that blind that he cannot see what is in front of his face? I had thought artists to have excellent powers of observation. What does he see in that mean-spirited, despicable woman?" She snapped her head in the other direction.

Cibo lifted her veil to reveal her pale and unpleasant face. Without saying a word, she showed the porter where to place her things, and then grabbed the arm of her companion, as if taking him into her possession.

Mme. Monier clasped my arm with her clammy hand. "Look. Over there: Blonskaya. How did she know? I do not envy her–or Cibo," she whispered.

Blonskaya, the other woman, dressed all in grey and using an umbrella like a cane, quickly walked up to the back of her artist, who sat motionless, staring into the mermaid eyes of his present companion. She spoke softly to him in Russian, "Sergei, what are you doing and where you are going? And why is it such a mystery for me, for all of us? Are you no longer our friend?" She began to weep quietly. "All the same, I know, and I know what it is leading to: your death! Perhaps I am to blame. Is there anything I can do to set things aright?"

"Oh, you think you can patch things up, do you?" Cibo hissed motionlessly, staring straight ahead, not at Blonskaya, as if she were blind.

"Would you stay, perhaps, if I married you? You know how much I love you," the woman in grey entreated as she rested a hand on his arm.

"No! No! No!" he screamed, pulling his arm away from Blonskaya. "I want nothing more to do with you!" His words felt disconnected, as if someone else had pressured him into speaking them. I could hear fear in his voice despite his strong protestations.

"Really? Is there nothing more I can do here to help you? Is this really the final curtain?" Tears began rolling down her cheeks.

"Perhaps it is," he spoke haltingly. "In any case, it is too late."

"Sergei, come to your senses!" Blonskaya continued to plead even though it was evident to the rest of us how hopeless it might be. "Come back because you will surely die, not only as an artist, but altogether." She began choking on her tears.

"What can I say? It is too late to fix anything," he cried, "and this is who I want!" He reached over and clasped Cibo's wrist, and her eerie eyes shifted to him.

"No!" Blonskaya shouted, "you do not want *that*!" she pointed at Cibo.

"How can you know what I want?" he yelled, slightly louder than before.

"I don't know," she said in a quieter tone. "What kind of man are you, Sergei?"

Cibo stood and followed the porter, who carried some of the suitcases. Without answering Blonskaya, the artist quietly stood up, put on his coat, picked up the portmanteau and joined his companion.

"So, Sergei, Sergei, you're going anyway?" The young woman sounded devastated.

Mme. Monier, chattered all the way to the boarding platform, then she said good-bye to all of us with hugs and *bisou* kisses. Once in her compartment, she glanced through the window and played at peek-a-boo with the bouquet of *Gloire de Dijon* roses, her brilliant red hair flashing and then disappearing. The train pulled off and Mme. Monier disappeared with it.

Back inside the waiting hall, we watched Blonskaya walk away quickly leaning on her umbrella.

The whole scene had been played like a tragic opera. "It's as if we were at a funeral," I observed.

"Some people feel that at every moment they are on their own," Stroop said to me without looking at me.

"I'm not sure I understand, Larion Dmitriyevich." Just saying his name made me smile.

"Even when you are surrounded by others," he looked away, "you can feel as if no one else in the world understands or appreciates you."

I thought back on my time at the Kazansky home, and subsequently with the Sorokins. Yes, people all around me, but I still felt singular and alone. I nodded my head in agreement.

"Many artists feel such solitude, as if they were hermits, even though they may be in the midst of an adoring crowd. Some even believe that if they died, no one would notice."

"When an artist dies, it can be very difficult." Was I starting to sound like Orsini? My attention got drawn away to the all-grey Blonskaya who had reached the way out and banged on the door with her umbrella to open it.

"Some people choose to live as an artist. Some do not." Stroop replied. "Their death is no less agonising."

"And it seems that sometimes there are things it is too late to do," I added as I turned my head toward the most handsome man in the room.

"Yes, sometimes there are things it is too late to do," repeated Stroop as his eyes met mine.

~ Π ~

That afternoon, Monsignor Mori asked if I would accompany him on a few errands. As we walked along, he would greet people as if he had known them for many years, but I could see in their faces they had no idea who this eccentric man might be. The two of us headed down to the footpath along the Arno.

We passed the Ponte Vecchio, with homes built right onto each side of the roadway, almost obscuring the old Roman arches. At the Galileo Museum, we turned and went up a wide street, stopping at a shop that had a sign with the picture of a fancy shoe hanging above it.

It was a short, little room, lit only by the open door. In one corner sat a round, old cobbler bent over a high boot with long laces. His glasses sat at the end of his nose, giving the impression of him having been in a painting by the Dutch master Gerrit Dou.

Inside, it was cool after being out in the hot sun on the street, and the room smelled of leather and jasmine. I looked about for the source of the flowery smell and saw a few twigs standing in a little bottle up near the ceiling on the top of a cabinet next to a pair of boots.

A young fellow wearing a leather cap and vest, whom I guessed was an apprentice, straddled a bench nearby, closely observing the master at work.

Mori cleared his throat, and when the cobbler looked up and saw the Monsignor, he set his tools down and wiped his sweaty hands with a red silk handkerchief.

"Vanya, this is Giuseppe, the creator of the most exquisite shoes in the world."

I smiled at him and he stood to hug Mori. "Monsignor! How good to see you. To what do I owe the pleasure?"

Mori looked down at me, "I was showing my young friend here around our beautiful little village and I thought he might like to meet you. I am sorry if we interrupted your work. Please, continue."

Old Giuseppe spoke melodiously and good-naturedly, "I, what? I am but a poor craftsman, *signori*, but there are artists, actors!" He produced a carafe from one of the cabinets, poured some chianti into a large glass and handed it to Mori, who accepted it without expressing thanks. "Oh, it is not so easy to make boots according to the rules of art. You need to know, to explore, the pace at which you sew. You need to know where the bone is wider, where there might be a corn, and where the rise is higher than it should be. After all, every man's feet are different from each other's, and you would be ignorant to think that the same shoes and boots would fit one and all alike."

He smiled at Mori, but the Monsignor continued to sip at the wine as if nothing else in the universe mattered.

"Everyone has feet, *signori*! And they all have to walk. The Lord God made it mandatory that one's feet have only five toes and a heel, and for everything else the same is true, you know? Yes, if a man had six toes on one foot, and four on the other–thus sayeth the Lord God endowed him with such feet–he would need to walk just as well as everyone else. Thank goodness I am a master shoemaker, and I know how to fashion such things."

Mori swallowed the last of the chianti with a loud gulp. He removed his broad black hat and swatted at the flies sitting on the top of a cabinet, where he set down the empty glass. His forehead was covered with sweat.

I looked over at the apprentice, who seemed to be catching up on his sleep during the expository speech by Giuseppe, whose even and melodious voice had a slightly soporific effect, as I found my own eyelids meeting now and again.

We left the cobbler's shop and continued to walk. As we rounded Cathedral Square near the Duomo, we met up with an elderly man wearing an obvious wig. His rouged cheeks stood out against his paper skin, and he practically leaned on two young girls who walked with him. The young women seemed somewhat modest, but with an air of authority. Mori informed me the aged gentleman was Count Guidetti.

I remembered some of the stories the Monsignor had told me about this dilapidated, old man, and his so-called "nieces." He also mentioned how the hoary lecher demanded such excitement for his dulled senses. Despite his advanced age and deathly, rouged face, he exhibited a shine of intelligence and wit, with still-lively eyes. I remembered some of the mumbled conversations which flew out of Mori's mouth, paradoxes of humour and stories, more and more of which had been lost over time. I recalled the voice of old Giuseppe, saying, "Yes, if a man had six toes on one foot, and four on the other–thus sayeth the Lord God endowed him with such feet–he would need to walk just as well as everyone else."

"The stone walls blushed when the Count confessed at his trial," Mori said as we passed to the left of a room filled with African spiritual figures and several lay visitors. "They prefer to fast on Fridays," he whispered and pointed at the worshippers.

An elderly Englishwoman walking with a beardless young man spoke with a strong accent, "We, the converted, we of the greater love, are more consciously appreciative of the beauty and charm of Catholicism, its rituals, its doctrines, its discipline."

I followed Mori into Caffè Giotto. "Poor woman," explained the Monsignor, as he put his hat on a wooden bench beside him. "She is from a rich, good family, but when she found the true faith, she felt she had to go out and preach to the needy. Everyone she knew began to recoil from her."

"Risotto! Three servings!" the waiter announced as he set three large bowls on the table in front of us. As we started to eat, a bottle of chianti appeared, and I picked at one bowl of the slimy rice dish as Mori gobbled down the rest.

"There were more than 300 of us pilgrims when we started from Pontassieve"–he took a swallow of the wine–"but by the time we reached Santissima Annunziata, there were always enough."

"St. George was certainly with him, and the Archangel Michael, and the Holy Virgin. With such protectors one cannot be afraid of anything in life!" I suddenly lost my presence of mind due to the general noise of the converted woman's English accent, who must have stopped just outside the entryway.

~ Π ~

Later, in the library, we continued my lessons. "He was born in Bithynia"–the Monsignor read to me from his notes like it was some kind of seminary lecture–"Bithynia in Asia Minor. It was much like Switzerland, with verdant hills, pristine streams running down from the mountains, and fertile pastures. He was a shepherd before he took up with his Emperor Hadrian. The boy accompanied the Emperor on journeys, including the one where he died in Egypt. Vague rumours floated about that he drowned himself in the Nile, like a sacrifice to the gods for the life of his patron. Others claimed that he drowned to save Hadrian while bathing. Coincidentally, the Egyptian god Osiris drowned in the same place on the same day of the year. At the hour of his death, astronomers reported they discovered a new star in the heavens. The circumstances of his demise have always been surrounded by an aura of mystery. The young man's extraordinary beauty affected not only the Emperor, and his presence at the Roman court revived an art movement that had previously come to a standstill. The inconsolable Emperor, wishing to honour his male favourite"–I could see trails of sweat trickling down the sides of the Monsignor's face–"elevated him to the rank of god, establishing honorary games, erecting gymnasiums and temples with oracles in his honour. During the first days after the boy's death, he wrote responses to ancient poems, glorifying his recently-departed lover."

He paused for a breath and wiped his brow with a cloth. "But it would be a mistake to think that this new cult was spread only by force. The assemblage of courtiers adopted this anointing as official and fell in with its founder. Almost a century later, we come across communities honouring Diana and Antinous whose sole purpose was to bury the members of the community, treat them to meals, provide charity, and modest services. Members of these congregations, ostensibly the first prototypes of Christianity, were people of the poorer classes until the subsequent institution of our modern religion. So, over time, the divinity of the Emperor's favourite stretched beyond the grave. He was a god of the night, quite popular among the poor. However, it did not spread very far, unlike the cult of Mithras, even though it was one of the strongest movements of a deified man."

He placed a thumb on the page to mark it, shut his notebook and looked at me over his glasses. "The morality of pagan emperors does not concern us, my son, but I cannot hide from you that the attitude of Hadrian to Antinous was, of course, not fatherly love."

This was not my first introduction to the topic of Hadrian and Antinous. Daniel Ivanovich had a bust of the Emperor's favourite in his St. Petersburg flat. An older man of power befriended a younger, handsome lad. Daniel Ivanovich referred to it as Sodomitic love, others have called it Pederasty. Why does this theme seem to keep arising in my life? Were people comparing me to the youthful beloved of Emperor Hadrian? My looks were certainly rare, but not to the level ascribed to the idolised Antinous.

"What made you decide to write about Antinous?" I asked the Monsignor, attempting to remain indifferent even though my curiosity had gotten the best of me once again.

"I read what you wrote this morning; however, I tend to write about the Roman Cæsars."

How amusing. He had also written about Tiberius and his time spent on Capri. Rumours abounded regarding the Emperor's sexual excesses and depravity. "Didn't you write about Tiberius, *cher père*?"

"Yes. I'm sure I have. What of it?"

"And about his life on Capri. Remember how the debauchery was described by Suetonius?"

Mori stiffened, as if I had struck an unpleasant nerve, and then he began to speak fervently, "Frightful! You are quite correct, my friend! It was frightful, and from his downfall, from this cesspool, only Christianity, the holy doctrine, made it possible to guide the human race!"

"But yet you feel more restrained about Emperor Hadrian's activities?"

"It's a big difference, my friend. There it is something sublime, although, after all, a terrifying delusion of feelings, a struggle which may not always be clear, even to people who have been enlightened by baptism."

"But, in fact, at any given moment, are they not one and the same?"

"You are perpetuating a terrifying misbelief, my son." He paused to wipe his sweaty brow again. "In every act, it is the attitude, its purpose, and the reasons that gave rise to it. Most actions are mechanical movements of our body, incapable of offending anyone, especially God."

He opened the notebook to the same page where his thick thumb had been placed and began to read silently.

~ Π ~

That evening, as I sat studying in my room by the light of an icon lamp, I heard voices drifting up the staircase from below. One, quite obviously Mori, the other less distinct. Setting aside the manuscript, I crept to the door but did not stick my head through the arch.

"It is your decision," Mori announced, as if he were providing advice to a judge. "No one else can help you. I'm sorry."

"Yes, I know." The second voice belonged to Stroop. What was he doing here? And why was he speaking with the Monsignor?

"I wish I could have been of more assistance, my friend. Is there anything else?"

Stroop coughed. "Please, do you have a scrap of paper and a pencil? I would like to leave a note."

"Of course." Mori's heavy shoes scuffed the stone floor, slowly getting softer, and then louder again. "Here you go."

"Thank you, Monsignor." For a few moments all I could hear was the sound of a pencil scratching on paper. "Here, deliver this for me, if you please."

"Anything for you, my friend."

I heard footsteps walking toward the front of the building, the gate opening and closing once more. Mori's heavy tramping approached, and I heard his footfall on the stairs. I rushed back to the manuscript and pretended to be studying intently.

"Vanya?" the Monsignor said as he reached the door, puffing for air.

"Oh, Monsignor, you surprised me," I prevaricated. "How may I be of assistance?"

His nose lifted so that his eyes could examine my choice of reading. "What is that you are studying?"

"Oh, this is a treatise on the Good Samaritan parable. You know, the travelling Samaritan comes across a beaten Jew on the road from Jericho to Jerusalem. Even though the Samaritans despise the Jews, this particular citizen stops to assist the beaten man to stand. The Jew tells him that a priest and a Levite had previously passed by and left him for dead. Then he asks the stranger, 'You are a Samaritan and I am a Jew. Why did you choose to help me when other members of my own faith would not?' and the Samaritan replies, 'Are you not my neighbour?'"

Mori coughed. "Yes, of course I know that story well. You did not need to tell it to me again." He held a piece of folded paper in one hand. The other supported his body against the door frame.

"Perhaps hearing it again is part of the heavenly plan, Monsignor." I know it sounded a bit uppity talking back to the priest who had been so gracious to host me, but the truth is the truth, no matter from whose mouth it escapes.

"Yes, well, I have something for you." He reached out the hand with the paper, and I walked to him and took it.

"Who is it from?" I asked even though I knew the answer.

Mori rolled his eyes heavenward. "I believe you know." We stood looking at each other, lingering, observing, expecting the other to move first. "Are you not going to look at the message?"

Of course I wanted to know what Stroop had written more than anything in the world. However, I was not certain that I wanted Mori to know the contents of the message. Then I realised he had probably read the note before walking up the stairs anyway.

I fumbled the paper open. The writing was in Russian. Perhaps the Monsignor could not have understood it after all. I looked up at him, and he stared back at me. The sensations I received from his gaze were kindness and caring, nothing more.

First I read the note to myself, and then aloud, "Vanya, please do me the honour of meeting me at the Via del Fosso Macinante entrance to Cascine Park tomorrow afternoon at four o'clock."

When I looked up at Mori's flushed face, a smile had appeared. He nodded gently to me.

"Good night to you, young Vanya. I believe tomorrow will be an especially auspicious day for you." He turned and began descending the treacherous stairs.

"Good night, Monsignor." I read the note a few more times before I tucked it inside my shirt, next to my heart. Yes, I believe that tomorrow shall be most auspicious, indeed.

~ П ~

I made sure I left the monastery in time to meet Stroop at the designated spot. Plenty of people passed by, and it reminded me of the days I would wait to catch a glimpse of Stroop in the Summer Garden of St. Petersburg. Back then I would sit on a bench and gaze at all the men as they walked. Even though I knew Larion Dmitriyevich wasn't in St. Petersburg at all, I went looking for him anyway. If a gentleman even looked slightly like Stroop I would watch him for as long as I could until he disappeared out of sight.

Standing on this particular corner, this very busy intersection, proved somewhat more difficult. Even though most of the bronzed, dark-haired men passing by looked nothing like my pale, blond Larion Dmitriyevich, there were more of them. However, in the past, my desire to find him was vague and unspecified. This meeting was requested by Stroop, and I needed to speak with him as much as I imagined he wanted to talk to me.

When he walked up my heart fluttered. This time it did not stand still.

"Hello, Vanya," he greeted me with a reassuring smile. "Thank you for meeting me here."

The lump in my throat would not move. I tried to speak, but no sound came. Instead, I did the only thing I could think of at the moment: I bowed slightly.

Stroop laughed out loud at the gesture. "Vanya, you can be so entertaining at times. Come along. Walk with me."

He extended his arm with a bare palm facing me. Was he asking me to grasp his hand? I have noticed many men in Italy walking hand-in-hand. Did he intend to offer friendship or something more?

When I did not reach out immediately, he jiggled his hand up and down to suggest that I take it, which I did. It felt big and warm, and I smiled.

We strolled along one of the paths through the garden, and through the imaginatively-manicured trees I could see farm meadows and low mountains behind them. We passed a restaurant, which was deserted at this time of the day. Mounds with circular patterns, and beds of blooming flowers caught my eye.

Soon we reached an incline where there were fewer people, and we moved along past an area with more views of the countryside. Guards with shiny buttons on their tunics sat on the benches at frequent intervals. A large, plump abbot attempted to supervise a group of boys running about on the leafy lawn.

Stroop stopped and sat on one of the benches. "I'm so grateful to you that you agreed to come here." He patted the empty seat next to him.

I was too nervous to sit. "I hope it wouldn't be discourteous of me to ask if we could continue to walk. I would rather, you know." His very presence made me lose the ability to complete a sentence.

"Very well." He stood and we began walking again, but not holding hands. Midway through a section of tall trees, he came to a stop, took a few more steps, then paused again. "Why have you deprived me of your friendship and your favour? Do you suspect me guilty in the death of Ida Goldberg?"

Had I said something about this to Daniel Ivanovich? I could not recall. "I did at first, but no longer. No."

"And why is it that you declined to continue our acquaintance? Please answer frankly." He turned his eyes on me, and I could tell no lies.

"I will answer frankly. It was because of your involvement with Fyodor." I wanted to look away, but I could not.

"Is that what you thought?"

"I know what happened, and you cannot deny it."

"No. Of course not." He was the one to look away first.

"Perhaps I would react very differently now, but back then I did not know much about anything. It has been very difficult because, I confess, I thought that I had lost you forever. No matter how silly it might seem now, I had hoped that you and I could be together in just the way you had described, according to the beauty of life."

I needed to step away because I felt embarrassed confessing my juvenile love to him. He caught up with me a moment later. The two of us walked, side-by-side, for a few minutes more.

We had made a complete circle around the lawn, and we started off again along the same path. A group of children played with a ball, and loud laughing echoed from far away.

Stroop stopped walking and turned to me. His face looked tight, as if he had something important to say to me.

"Tomorrow I have to go, in this case, down to Bari, but I could just as easily stay. It now depends on you."

That seemed like a great deal of pressure for a love-struck teenager to deal with. He gave me the power to control his actions, should he abide by his statement.

"You would change your plans for me?"

"Yes," he swallowed, "Yes, I would."

Not knowing how to respond to his generous offer, I inhaled deeply and sighed with a slight whine. I looked up at him with a tear in one eye only to see him tearing up as well.

"I shall visit the monastery tomorrow morning." He pulled out his pocket square and dabbed first at his face then at mine. "You can leave a note with Monsignor Mori if you no longer wish to see me. Should the answer be 'No,' and you desire me to leave and never bother you again, write, 'Go,' but if the answer is 'Yes,' and you want to be part of my life, write, 'Stay'."

This arrangement confused me. "So then is 'no' a 'yes'?"

He sighed plaintively. "Do you want me to make some kind of promise to you?" The handkerchief returned to its pocket.

"No, no, no. I suppose I understand. But why are you putting it this way?"

"I believe this is the way it has now become necessary. I was just waiting for the proper opportunity."

I guess he needed to see if my feelings for him had changed permanently.

"I shall answer you either way." Saying that made me feel more grown-up than anything I had done up to that point.

He smiled. "I think that with just one more effort, you will grow your wings, I can already see them."

I looked over my shoulder to see if there were, indeed, little wings.

"Perhaps, but I imagine it will be more painful as they grow," I said with a grin.

Without saying anything more, we both turned and started walking back to the monastery.

~ Π ~

When I got back, Hugo Orsini had stopped by to call upon Monsignor Mori. The two sat at the communal table eating and talking.

"Ah! Young Vanya," Mori called out. "How was your interview with Stroop?"

Disclosing the intimate nature of our conversation to them was probably the last thing I wanted to do. However, I could not ignore the question either. "We walked around the garden and discussed some plans for the future."

"Oh! So you shall be travelling with Larion Dmitriyevich after all," Orsini deduced from my veiled statement.

"Well, not exactly. He shared his plans with me, and then he invited me to join him."

"That sounds wonderful!" Mori gushed. Perhaps he wished me gone after all. "When are you leaving?" The question made me feel no longer welcome in his monastery; however, I really hadn't contributed much to it anyway.

"That has not yet been decided, and I don't even know if I will be joining him." I looked back and forth between them, making eye contact with each in turn.

"Oh, but you must!" Orsini burst out, and then Mori joined in for the repetition, "You must!"

At least I knew where I stood in Florence. Once again, the poor orphan that no one wanted. Since the death of my mother, I have had to live at the whim and generosity of others. None of these places has felt like home to me, and it seems I have always made the choice to go, rather than to stay, in hopes of discovering that the other side of the river would be more pleasant than the one I left behind. Although at times it felt like I merely jumped from fire to flame.

"Are you hungry, Vanya?" Mori asked. "Please sit with us. *Signor* Orsini was just sharing with me his ideas for a new work, one with dramatic settings and mythological allegory. I believe you might enjoy this."

Yes, I was hungry, but listening to Hugo drone on about his theatrical visions would be the exacting price I would have to pay for the meal.

As I picked at some cheese and dried meat, Orsini waxed on, "I have yet to decide on a name for my heroine, but this is what you would see as the curtain opened: the gray sea, rocks, a distant golden sky beckoning." His hands flew about, indicating the placement of the scenery. "Perhaps it will be comparable to the Argonauts in their search for the Golden Fleece. It will all be frightening in its novelty and unprecedented. Suddenly, they discover love in their ancient homeland."

I remembered this theme from Stroop's long speech about Hellenes. He even referred to the assembled company as Argonauts.

"All very interesting, Hugo," Mori said with a surreptitious wink to me. "Vanya, would you like some wine?"

I held up an empty cup from the table and the Monsignor filled it halfway.

"Yes, but that is only the first act!" Orsini smiled like a Cheshire Cat. "In the second act we see Prometheus, chained and punished. He sings, 'No one can behold with any certainty or impunity the secrets of nature without violating its laws. Only by killing one's father, having incestuous relations with one's mother and guessing the riddle of the Sphinx can one attain this knowledge!' Pasiphæ appears, blinded with obsession for the bull, dreadful and prophetic, and she sings, 'I see no patchwork of disorderly life, no coherent life or prophetic visions of harmony.' Everything is in disaster!" His arms swivelled about in a mechanical demonstration of chaos.

"That is truly amazing, master," Mori purred like a true sycophant, and then turned to me. "Don't you think so, Vanya?" His exaggerated expression communicated a suggestion to shine Orsini on.

"Oh, yes, Monsignor. I can truly say I have never heard or seen anything like that." At least I was not lying. The whole concept sounded as tumultuous as the very scenes he described. "Perhaps when you are producing your new work, the Monsignor and I can attend." I smirked at Mori, and he rolled his eyes skyward.

"Oh, but you have not heard the last of it!" Hugo spoke with such passion, a fusillade of saliva sprayed across the table. Mori and I exchanged knowing glances. "In the third act, we are in the blessed forest, like a scene from Ovid's 'Metamorphoses,' where the gods have received all love from all kinds of creatures. Icarus falls to his death. Phæton falls to his death. And then Ganymede sings, 'Poor brethren, only I can soar through the sky and remain there. Because you are drawn to the sun with your pride and your childish toys, I have adopted a vociferous love incomprehensible to mortals.' Prophetically huge flowers burst forth with fiery blossoms. Birds and animals walk two-and-two as a pulsating pink fog creeps onto the stage. Out of the billowing fog emerges 48 examples of human conjugation from the Indian *Manuels Érotiques*."

Mori's eyebrows practically shot off the top of his head, and I had to fight to keep from laughing at the spectacle.

"And everything starts spinning in a double rotation–each in its own sphere! And inside the great circle, everything whirls faster and faster, while the whole thing coalesces together and the entire moving mass rearranges itself and comes to an abrupt halt on a treeless, yellow precipice above the sparkling sea." His sparkling eyes portrayed the very passion he was attempting to describe. "As the unbearable sun sets behind the unrelenting cliff, we see revealed the huge radiant figure of Zeus-Dionysus-Helios!"

Hugo smiled beatifically at each of us in turn. Mori and I looked to each other, and then the Monsignor began to applaud and I joined in.

~ Π ~

That evening, after Orsini finally left (the food and wine had run out), I realised I needed to spend some solitary time in order to consider my options with Stroop. I climbed up to the rarely-used balcony at the top of the monastery. From that vantage I could see most of Florence laid out before me. Blasts from a train whistle interrupted the twilight calm. Lights began to appear from various buildings in a seemingly random pattern. Stars in the heaven also started to shine, also in a seemingly random pattern.

The randomness of these occurrences made me think back upon the apparent random events in my own life. Until my mother died, I had led a very sheltered and predictable life in a small village in the middle-of-nothing Russia. Upon her death, I got sent to the Kazansky circus in St. Petersburg. Through them I met Larion Dmitriyevich Stroop, the first man I had ever fallen in love with. At school, I met Daniel Ivanovich, the first man who had ever taken a healthy interest in my education. Ida Goldberg tutored me in the Classics and expanded my mind even further. It all seemed so random looking back from my current vantage point: the chance meetings, the unintended happenstances. However, revelations regarding Stroop's activities in the Turkish bath, and the subsequent apparent suicide of Ida Goldberg, turned my heart.

When an opportunity to leave St. Petersburg presented itself, I leapt at the chance to escape the distressing town and the Kazanskys (even though two of their ilk ended up following me all the way to the banks of the Volga River).

During the months I lived with the Sorokins, I learned how it felt to perform hard, physical labour. Working in their orchard and assisting with the crops taught me many valuable lessons. However, when the mother attempted to force me into having intimate relations against my wishes, I knew it was time to leave, but I had nowhere to go.

Fortunately, my old Greek teacher, Daniel Ivanovich, had appeared out of nowhere with a family inheritance. He offered to show me around Italy, and once again I jumped at the chance to escape my latest predicament.

I have been exposed to various institutions of religion, from the Ancient Greeks to the Old Believers, to Russian Orthodox, and then Roman Catholicism. None of these systems really appealed to me very much. None of them provided the confidence to pursue my life in the way I wanted to experience it.

More than any philosophy or religion, it had been opera that provided much of my morality. Observing larger-than-life characters fight with their demons, whether external or internal, demonstrated a sense of resolve necessary for a successful life. They fought for their loves, sometimes to the death, but that only helped to prove the power of such a universal emotion.

One constant theme for me the whole time has been my fascination with Stroop. Throughout all of these experiences, his presence remained significant, sometimes sweet radish and at other times, horseradish. And I needed to make a decision in a very short time that could affect the rest of my entire adult life.

To stay here in Florence with him seemed the obvious choice. He said he was willing to set aside his travel plans to remain with me. But what did I have to offer him? It seemed unfair that I should be getting all the benefits and he got none. In fact, depriving him of his travelling affairs would seem to be a detriment in itself. However, he offered, and it would be foolish to pass up such a once-in-a-lifetime opportunity.

On the other hand, I was still young. There would be many other opportunities available to me. Plenty of Fyodors, Sashas, and Daniels awaited me wherever I went. Perhaps Stroop was not the perfect man for me after all. He could tire of me–or me of him–in a week, a month, a year. Unfortunately, if I chose this option, I would then be responsible for my own room and board, and I was not quite ready to be financially independent.

Living with Larion Dmitriyevich would have alleviated the need to earn money, but then I would have been beholden to him for my very existence. It was all so complicated! Each choice had its advantages and disadvantages. Each path twisted about in my mind like a kaleidoscopic garden nightmare. A labyrinth of hedges, lakes, flowerbeds, and playgrounds stood between me and my ultimate judgment.

By the time I had finally arrived at a decision, the dawn, bright, almost-poisonous, cracked the sky. Again, I found myself weighing what I wanted to do against what I needed to do. I climbed down from the balcony and back to my room where I took up a piece of paper and an ink pen. I scrawled my response, waved my hand over it to dry the ink, then folded it once.

The rickety wooden stairs announced my early-morning arrival on the ground floor, but no one else had as yet arisen. I placed the note on the table by the courtyard door and crept back up to my bed, where I hoped to get some rest before the busy day ahead of us all began.

~ Π ~

Opening and closing of the front gate woke me. My head sloshed with wine from the previous evening, and a dull pounding started working its way from back to front.

I jumped to the basin and splashed water on my face. Looking back in the mirror was a baggy-eyed youth with delicate eyebrows and unkempt hair. Brushing the unruly Medusa-like coiffure did not help much, but the result was not as scary as when I had started.

The crumpled shirt I wore yesterday was closest to me. I slipped into in it and tip-toed down the stairs just to the point where I could spy Stroop standing by the courtyard door with my note in his hand.

He stared at the single word on the front piece, "Go!" His head turned left, then right. Then he opened the folded paper to see what I had added inside, "I shall go with you. Vanya."

Behind me I found a set of weather-beaten wooden shutters. I threw them open, and suddenly the ancient courtyard below flooded with bright sunshine. The sisters, like the proverbial choir of angels, began singing their morning prayers.

Stroop ran to the stairs and took the first step. I flew down the rest of the way as if I had at long last sprouted my wings. We embraced and kissed for the very first time, but certainly not for the very last.

Part Four
Vanya says, Stay! (Оставайтесь)

THAT AFTERNOON WE LEFT FOR BARI, a train ride I would never forget. Even though we hardly spoke, I focused more on my travelling partner than the passing Italian hills and Apennines. By the time we reached the Adriatic coast, night had fallen, and we went directly to our rooms off Piazza Umberto, a few blocks from the train depot.

It was there on the warm shores of the Mediterranean Sea that I first enjoyed the company of another man in an intimate way. Once we had secured the door and windows, Larion Dmitriyevich removed my clothing and had me stand naked before him. The smile on his face was all I needed. Adolescent nature took over, and my body responded accordingly.

He took me to the bed and pleasured us both in the way that only two men could enjoy. I fell asleep happier than I had ever been, and I secretly pledged to be with him for the rest of my life.

In the morning, we took a carriage to a *circolo* called Molo Vecchio that plunged out into the sea. The architecture seemed more Eastern European, with its onion-shaped dome, Greek Orthodox cross, and icon panels. Each façade of the gazebo contained a high, rounded archway with a decorative crest above it.

We ate a light breakfast, rented bathing costumes and took a plunge. Unlike the chilly Volga, the Adriatic Sea warmed my skin, and its saltiness kept me more buoyant. Its distinctive blue colour also tantalised my eyes. I had never seen this particular hue, somewhat darker than the blue in the French flag, but with a very slight green tint to it.

After a while, the area became overpopulated with other bathers, and we headed back to the shore. The small, green-blue waves reflected sunlight off their tips and seemed to be devouring the sand like an amphibious assault.

Stroop wanted me to return to our rooms while he conducted his business, but I convinced him to let me stay at the beach. I told him I would walk back in time to meet him for our evening meal.

While not as picturesque as Rome or Florence, Bari had its own quaint charm. Many buildings had plain vertical sides but with arch-shaped windows near the top, lending a more modern look. After a while I realised another difference: the buildings tended to be taller and closer together than in the other Italian cities. This arrangement caused more shadows during the day, especially along the streets that ran north-to-south.

I peered into shops along the way (chemists, bakeries, clothiers, florists), but with no pocket money, purchases were out of the question. However, as in Rome and Florence, the Italians I encountered appeared intrigued by my traditional Russian peasant costume.

"Eh, *signor*," I would hear, "where are you from?"

Because I did not know them, and they did not know me, I figured a little harmless fiction would not hurt anyone. "I am a travelling prince from Russia." Mouths would purse and eyes would bulge at the idea of meeting visiting royalty. One caffè owner begged me to sit at the table closest to the sidewalk so that tourists would think his was the best place to go, given that a person of my presumed nobility patronised his establishment. Coffee and ice cream kept appearing unbidden until I finally got him to accept that I needed to leave.

"And how was the rest of your day," Stroop asked over the meal in our hotel room.

I explained my tour of the area, including posing as the Travelling Prince.

"Be careful, my *drozdik*," he said sternly but with concern, "the caffè proprietor might have become quite angry if he discovered your deception."

Drozdik, he called me: "little thrush." I suppose that would be fairly appropriate and somewhat amusing.

"No one else in all of Bari knows me, save you," and I plucked another sardine from the platter and swallowed it whole. Just as I reached for the bowl of turnip tops to get another serving, Stroop grasped my hand firmly.

"Vanya, this is all new to you. Please realise that not everywhere we go will people treat you with unwarranted dignity." His eyes communicated caring more than scolding.

"Yes, Larion Dmitriyevich. I know I was being foolish, but it was such grand fun." I smiled at him and he smiled back.

"Well, try to behave yourself, especially in new and unfamiliar settings. Some of these people are scheming and conniving, and they will want to take your money and your valuables."

"But I have neither money nor valuables! What would they want with me?" I had not yet learned the ways of the world, and I wanted everyone around me to be generous and interesting.

"Please, Vanya, listen to what I am trying to tell you. There are evil people in every shadow who would think nothing of dispatching your lovely figure if it suited their need."

"Then I will avoid those shadows and remain only in the light." I thought back to the previous morning and the cascade of sunlight that bathed the courtyard of the monastery in Florence.

Stroop pressed his lips together tightly, and he appeared distressed about something.

"I know you have enjoyed your time in Italy," he said at length, "but I have received a request to leave this country. How would you like to visit Egypt?"

"Egypt?! Would I!" How exciting it would be to walk in the footsteps of the pharaohs and climb their pyramid burial structures.

"I need to remain in Alexandria for a month or so, but I have concerns about your continuing education. Would you willing to attend a school there?"

"Alexandria? How far is that from Luxor?"

"Oh, over 200 *versta*, but much of the rest of the world uses a different measurement system."

"Yes, the Metric System. Monsignor Mori made sure I knew how to see the world in metres, litres and kilograms."

"Very good. Then I would say that Luxor is about 200 kilometres from Alexandria. Why do you ask?"

My head tilted to one side in frustration that he had no clue as to my interest in the Valley of the Kings. "Well, I would like to see the Sphinx and the Nile River and the pyramids there."

"Oh, yes, of course," he chuckled to himself. "I am not sure we will have time for such exploration, but I understand your curiosity."

"Have you seen the Sphinx?"

"When I was young, my parents brought me to observe the ancient Egyptian relics, but I tell you, I would imagine the Sphinx looked much better before Napoleon Bonaparte." He winked and touched his nose with a finger, and we both burst out laughing.

~ Π ~

The next morning, I wrote to Nata, explaining how Stroop had invited me to tour with him. I hoped she would read my letter and turn completely red with envy. The man she had hoped to marry had chosen me over her. I had also considered writing "Uncle" Nika to explain that he need not pay the Kazanskys any longer, but, somehow, time escaped me. I was sure that at some point he would make good on his promise to call on me at St. Petersburg, and he would discover for himself that he had been paying those bourgeois rogues needlessly.

Two days later we boarded a vessel bound for Alexandria. I had no idea what to expect, never having been on a ship of that size. The last time I travelled by water, with the ghastly Kazanskys, there was not much to see or do.

Once our ship cleared the Italian Peninsula, no land could be seen in any direction. It was the first time I was completely at sea, and I began to panic.

Larion Dmitriyevich took my hand and guided me back to our cabin and sat with me on the bed until I calmed sufficiently. After that, I slowly conditioned myself to life on the open waters, and I quickly went back to hanging over the rail to catch the spectacular views.

The waves on the open sea appeared to be much larger that the ankle-height ones at Bari. Some looked to be taller than Stroop. The sunlight sparkled on the crests, flashing a secret, coded message to anyone who might understand.

At the times when the water remained calm, it glimmered like the light on church windows, as if some ancient artist created a horizontal masterpiece of intersecting coloured shards.

For a few days Stroop was the only person I spoke with. As the ship meandered southward toward the African coast, he and I interacted with almost no one else. No crazy relatives, no zealous religious fanatics, no self-important minor Italian aristocrats, no pompous priests, no lovesick artists. I did miss the nights at the opera, however. Without these distractions, it gave us the time to get to know each other in a way we had not previously.

We would stand at the stern watching the ripples in the water behind the boat just talking and sharing our stories. As the sun began to drop below the western horizon, the water would glow from beneath, as if the sea itself had swallowed the great ball in the sky. It was Poseidon conquering Helios for the night with only Selene, in her celestial silver chariot, to guide us. *We are Dionysians! We are Argonauts! We are Hellenes!*

My thoughts drifted to Daniel Ivanovich, my old Greek teacher, whom I last saw in Rome. When he first told me of his inheritance at Vasilsursk, he listed off a few places he wanted to visit, and I seemed to remember that Alexandria was one of them. I did hope we would meet up, especially if it was once again by chance.

As we approached Alexandria, I could see it had been built on a strip of land that jutted out into the Mediterranean Sea. Like a bony finger, it pointed the arriving traveller toward the west. "Go *that* way!" it beckoned, "Don't come ashore here!"

When we docked at the port, a gentleman in a huge turban wearing a flowing robe greeted us on the quay, bowing to us both with clasped hands.

"*Sadiqi* Stroop. How nice of you to afford us with your acquaintance once more." He turned and eyed me. "And who is your delightful companion?" Another bow, but just to me. I still wore the Russian peasant costume, and he must have mistaken me for royalty.

"This is Vanya, my... my... gentleman friend."

My pained expression must have surprised both men. Stroop and I had not formally discussed our relationship nor what words we could use in describing it to others.

"*Salaam*, Vanya. I am Zahi, your guide while you are in Alexandria." He indicated a cart nearby. It was rather plain and boxy. Even my "Uncle" Kostya had a better-looking cab. I looked to Stroop and he climbed in as though it were the Tsar's royal coach. The three of us rode past the slaughterhouse and the tanneries, a statue of Mohamed Ali, a column dedicated to Alexander, and Pompei's Pillar (a lone, remaining reminder of the Romans sited near a miniature rendition of the Sphinx). Alexandria proved to be the smelliest place I had ever visited. After 20 minutes, we arrived at our hotel on the other side of the peninsula.

~ Π ~

Zahi, our guide, accompanied me any time I left the hotel. He walked with me to school in the morning, and he waited faithfully outside at the end of the day. Apparently, Stroop thought I was not yet self-reliant.

One afternoon, as I walked with Zahi back to our hotel, I heard strange cries piercing the air of the otherwise noisy, crowded, smelly street. It stopped briefly but then started up again, like a mixture of a buzzing hornet and a bleating sheep. "Zahi, what is that sound?"

He raised his eyebrows, and squinted as he listened. "Oh, that is a muezzin."

"A muezzin? Do you eat them?"

The Egyptian burst out in knells of laughter. "Oh, my dear boy"–he managed to say once he regained control–"a muezzin is a *who*, not a *what*!" His amused smile remained. "He is a cleric who delivers the *adhan*, the call to worship. Ever since the time of Bilal ibn Ribah, who walked the streets of Mecca calling the faithful to prayer and to witness the words of the Prophet Muhammad, every mosque has had a muezzin."

"I am so sorry. He is an Arab, then?"

"Perhaps. Not all Arabs follow the Prophet."

"Then he is a Muhammadan?"

"Yes. Would you like to attend the prayer? It is open to all, regardless of their faith."

I had only witnessed the religious practises of the Catholics up to that point. We had the time, and I had the curiosity. "Yes, please. I would very much enjoy that."

Zahi smiled, grasped my hand and led me to a nearby mosque, splendid in its design and appointments. I noticed how the intricate designs worked into the walls were stylised Arabic writing. Many of the decorations held jewels and colourful tiles. What I did not see were icons of their saints and prophets.

Before entering the main sanctuary, Zahi sat down and began removing his shoes. He glanced up at me and said in a sub-dued tone, "Shoes are not permitted inside the prayer hall."

After we finished taking our footwear off, he stood up and led me to a bowl of water, not very different from a holy water font, where he took handfuls of water and dribbled it over his face. Then he nodded his head toward the vessel, suggesting I do the same. I had already been baptised, and I didn't think this ritual would cause my soul any more harm.

Inside the prayer hall, rectangular carpets filled the floor, all pointing in the same direction. Zahi indicated an alcove and wiggled his finger, which I took to mean that was where I should go.

He stepped to one of the carpets and began his prayer ritual with about a dozen other worshippers. Together, they stood and prayed, bowed and prayed, knelt and prayed, sat and prayed. The cycle repeated, and then Zahi returned to me.

"What did you think, young master?" he asked as we donned our shoes.

"I found it curious that the congregants conducted their prayers all by themselves. In our church, the priest leads the worship, and we follow along like lambs."

The Arab smiled. "That is because we are free to practise our faith independently."

"I see. That sounds more democratic than our hierarchal system." He nodded. "By the way, why do you not show the images of your saints and prophets in the church? At home, everywhere we go there are statues and paintings, frescoes and windows depicting our icons."

Zahi's eyes went wide. "Young master, it is forbidden to represent living beings in art. That would be considered *shirk*... how to say... that would be idolatry and a diversion from the one true god, Allah."

How strange it would have been to enter a church or cathedral and not seen the icons I had grown up with. It would have been most difficult for the Old Believers, as they seemed quite attached to their icon lamps, statues and relics.

Weeks went by, and I attended a nearby Secondary School for foreigners. Classes were taught in a variety of languages, including: Greek, Arabic, Latin, French, and English. As I had already studied most of them, it was not difficult to fit in and gain favour with the instructors.

The Arabic language proved most difficult. All the others had some relation to each other through linguistic commonalities; however, Arabic had almost no cognates, and I had to learn that awfully-harsh, throat-clearing consonant. In addition, they write backwards, making it terribly inconvenient. My wrist kept dragging the wet ink across the page until someone finally showed me how to use the little finger as a hand rest.

After a while, Alexandria began to look even more like a thieves' den than the upstairs tavern in San Lorenzo run by the buxom Pasca. The architecture merged ancient Egyptian, Greek and Roman with Moorish arches and spires. Even with open sky, the salty smell of the sea, and its bustling market-place, I felt that at any moment one of the dark-skinned men might snatch me away for a ransom. It surprised me that no one had yet penned an opera that took place in this clamorous, malodourous, eclectic metropolis.

~ Π ~

In the evenings, after the torrid heat of the day subsided, Larion Dmitriyevich, Zahi, and I would walk about, allowing me to get a better sense of Alexandria. Partly modern, partly ancient, it was a city at odds with itself. The charming veneer of Middle-Eastern culture and design barely concealed its desire to compete with Cairo and Port Said for shipping business. Some days I would have Zahi take me by the port on the way home, and we would stand on a quay to watch the large vessels sail in, sail out, or sail by.

I had precious little time alone, as I was either with Stroop, Zahi, or my classmates. None of the teachers inspired me the way Daniel Ivanovich did, but I learned my lessons, nonetheless.

One evening Stroop brought me to meet a friend of his, a poet. "Connie," as Larion Dmitriyevich called him, treated us to a lavish feast at his home on the other side of Alexandria. He sported a heavily-waxed moustache that turned up at the ends, and his spectacles sat on his nose with no ear pieces to secure them. The oily, browned skin on his face seemed more like leather with large pores. His dark hair had been slicked back with pomade and covered with a round, pointed, ornate cap trimmed with colourful brocade.

When Stroop introduced us, Connie stared at me for a few seconds and then turned to Larion Dmitriyevich, "Lary, darling, your taste is exquisite. Wherever did you find him, and can you get one like him for me?" He laughed daintily, like a girl.

Stroop's face reddened. "Sorry, Connie. As with all my acquisitions and wares, I never divulge my sources."

Acquisitions and wares? Was that what I was to him after all this time?

"Come, let us eat together, and perhaps I can lure the boy away from you." He smiled primly, making the ends of his moustache nearly touch the sides of his bulbous nose.

As we followed our host into the white stone courtyard, I looked up at Stroop. "Even though you may think of me as nothing more than an acquisition, I assure you there is nothing this man could do to lure me away from you."

He squeezed my shoulder. "Vanya, I regret the remark, but Connie is very influential and is used to getting whatever he wants. Please accept my apologies."

I looked up with a pout. "Taking me to Luxor might make up for it, you know."

He slapped me playfully on the side of the head, propelling me toward the table. "Like they used to say in Ancient Rome: Acquisitions should be seen and never heard!"

Half a dozen other people joined with us to dine, and we sat on tall, tufted pillows around a low table. The women wore bejewelled, pastel veils over their faces, but you could still see exotic cosmetics beneath. Their gauzy gowns gave me the impression they might have been more at home in a seraglio, and strains of Mozart played through my head. The men wore full-length white robes with either elaborate turbans or tasselled, felt fezzes. At last I felt my Russian peasant costume no longer stood out in the crowd.

Over dinner, Connie recited poetry he had written. It was in Greek, but I could understand most of it. Here is a segment I recalled:

> *When you depart for Ithaca,*
> *Wish for the road to be long,*
> *Full of adventure, full of knowledge.*
> *Don't fear the Læstrygonians and the Cyclops,*
> *Or the angry Poseidon.*

His poetry evoked the memories of classes with Daniel Ivanovich. It was then that I realised I longed for his companionship, and I hoped he was off enjoying himself wherever he might be in this wonderful world.

As Connie continued to recite his lurid verses, he waltzed about the space, stopping to lay his hands on the various guests of both sexes. When he approached me, Stroop gave him a stern glance, and he passed me by.

At the conclusion of his saga, which spoke of many types of love, both with men and women, I moved to clap my hands in appreciation. Larion Dmitriyevich grabbed my wrist and shook his head. Instead of applauding, people around the table began humming, creating a sound that resembled a swarm of angry bees. A most peculiar custom.

One of the servers brought a tray with glasses and a bottle of a milky, pale golden liquid. She poured each of us a portion and set in on the table in front of us.

"What is that?" I whispered to Stroop.

"Thibarine, an after-dinner apéritif."

When all the guests had received their glass, Connie stood, lifted his in the air and proclaimed, "To friends and to love, in all its varieties." He looked directly at us and then downed his drink.

I sipped at the strange-looking liquid. It smelled sweet, but its taste proved unfamiliar. At first it seemed like *tmina*, what others called caraway. Then, the unmistakable tang of cardamom, and finally, the syrupy flavour of dates. When the servant made a second round, I quickly held up my glass for a top-off.

"Be careful, Vanya," Stroop warned, "it is very strong. Keep your head, please."

No matter what it was, it helped getting through the evening much easier. Connie kept batting his eyes at me, and Larion Dmitriyevich would then position himself between us.

Dancing women with spangled strands of medallions undulated seductively around the table. Through the pale gauze covering much of their bodies, I saw gems in navels, gems on tassels, gems on fingers, gems on just about every part of the body where a gem could be. They whirled and gyrated, their hips seeming to vibrate continuously.

Our host attempted to move through the dancers' formation, but they deftly avoided any physical contact with him and moved strategically around. The colours, the lights, the exotic music all swirled in my head as the Thibarine sloshed about.

At some point, I fell asleep, and I didn't recall the carriage ride back to the hotel.

~ Π ~

A few days later, while we ate our evening meal of figs and cheese, Zahi appeared. "*Sadiqi* Stroop, I have an urgent communiqué for you from England." Larion Dmitriyevich reached into his pockets and pulled out a few coins to give our guide. "*Shukran, shukran.* You shall most assuredly be most blessed in heaven, *sadiqi* Stroop."

Once Zahi had left, Larion Dmitriyevich opened the letter and began to read. At first his face held a smile, but then it faded until he finally tossed his head back sharply in dismay.

"Bad news?" I mumbled through some half-eaten cheese.

"Of a sort," he replied. "A friend in London has asked me to call upon him."

"London?" I began envisioning palaces, the Thames River and the Tower. "Yes, please." Alexandria had been fun, exotic and educational, but it had also been hot, muggy, and interminably malodourous. Perhaps the English capital would also be safer for a lad my age, and I would be able to walk about on my own again without a minder.

Stroop chuckled at my audacity. He would be the one having to pay for our transport, room and board, but I was the one to force his hand. "Yes, London it is, my *drozdik*."

"So who is this mysterious friend? A former lover, perhaps?" I coyly placed a finger on my lips and darted my eyes.

"No!" came the sharp reply, "nothing of the sort. He is an old school chum. We sat at university together."

"I see. And why the sudden request for your particular company?"

He paused and thought before responding, "I'm not really sure, but his writing suggests urgency. The fact that he sought me out is nearly reason enough. While England is generally a lovely place with lovely people, their morals are not as... how can I put this?... tolerant of difference as other cultures we have experienced or studied. A few centuries back they suffered a wave of self-inflicted temperance called 'Puritanism' led by some of their overzealous Protestant ministers. Many of the pleasurable, hedonistic acts we enjoy today would have been labelled 'un-godly' and persecuted."

I shuddered. "How quaint and old-fashioned."

"But the Puritans came to power and enacted laws that are still enforced today, and that is the concern I have regarding my friend."

"And his name, if you please?"

Stroop smiled, "Royall Allen-Wilson, but I call him Roy."

"Royall Allen-Wilson?" my voice went shrill. "What kind of name is that?"

"Well..."–Larion Dmitriyevich exhaled loudly–"he is descended from the kings of Scotland, which makes him a relative of the English King Edward, and, incidentally, our beloved Tsar Nikolay Alexandrovich."

"That explains the Royall part, but what of Allen... what was it?"

"Allen-Wilson."

"Is that a patronymic name?"

"Not exactly. The British do not use a patronymic, but frequently, when great houses join, the mother's name is affixed with a hyphen. As an example, if my mother had held a titled position, my name would have been Orloff-Stroop."

"And I would have been Mishkin-Smurov. Quite a mouthful, I say."

"As if Ivan Igorevich is not?"

"Not at all, Larion Dmi-tri-ye-vich," I stressed the individual syllables, and we both smiled before falling into each other's arms for an evening of physical pleasure.

Within a week, Stroop concluded his dealings in Egypt, and we were on a steamer to England. At least this ship kept closer to land, and I spent most of my days once again hanging onto the rail watching the scenery float by.

After a few days of seeing so many similar landscapes go past, I began thinking of rhymes, silly little rhymes at first. Inspired by our evening with Connie, I began carrying paper and pencil with me everywhere I went on-board. Jotting down simple couplets became one of the main sources of entertainment.

Most exciting to me was the Strait of Gibraltar, where I conjured up an image of Scylla and Charybdis. Unlike the monsters in the story, these shores gazed at each other across over 14 kilometres of water, but I was still able to see them both. Much like Homer's Odysseus, I stared at each cliff in turn, imagining which would be the correct, or incorrect, choice; for if I erred in judgment, the ship would be lost entirely. Fortunately, the captain remained steady, and we forged out into the open Atlantic.

Another thrilling aspect for me was the coast of Portugal. All along the way I could see ancient castles looming along the shore. Visions of voracious pirates and intrepid explorers filled my head. In my mind, I saw armies with tall trebuchets, sturdy siege engines, and crossbows attempting wave upon wave to topple each fortress in their way.

After that, it was mostly farms and farmland until we reached Dover, when the frighteningly tall chalk bluffs loomed above us.

Sailing up the Thames felt like Odysseus returning to Ithaca. Not only did the blue, pulsating water remind me of the nostalgic Mediterranean, people lined the shores, waving and cheering as we pulled up to the moorings. A proper hero's welcome with banners and bunting.

Standing among the crowd at the gangway was a rather tall, clean-shaven, coppery-haired fellow in a prim, grey suit smiling at Stroop.

"Is that your friend?" I pointed.

"Yes. That is Roy."

Oh, no. Yet another ginger. I prayed that his temperament would be far superior to the mercurial frog we had left behind in Russia.

~ Π ~

Mr. Allen-Wilson hired a cab along the strand and instructed the driver to take us to Piccadilly Circus. London reminded me more of Florence, as it was not very tall, and every so often a tower or spire broke the line of rooftops.

As we approached the grand circular plaza, the cab passed a bronze statue of a winged boy shooting arrows from atop a fountain.

"They say if you sit on the stairs long enough"–Mr. Allen-Wilson informed me–"you will eventually find your true love."

"Well"–Larion Dmitriyevich coughed–"he won't be needing that, I can assure you," and he smiled at me.

They were speaking in English, and I am glad that Stroop prepared me for this. Without his assistance, the conversation might as well have been as incomprehensible as Arabic.

"Is that Eros?" I asked.

"No, oddly enough. Most people mistake it for Eros, but it is actually Anteros, his lesser-known brother. He is the god of unrequited love."

"Even though Anteros has wings just like his brother, he obstructs the happiness of others," I observed. "How sad."

"Yes, how sad," Stroop echoed.

The cab stopped in front of Lyons Corner House, a coffee shop in Coventry Street. Its front rounded the corner of Piccadilly, and the façade looked to have been cut from limestone, similar to many of the buildings in St. Petersburg.

We stepped inside and a hostess in a black uniform approached us. "Your usual table, Mr. Allen-Wilson?" she inquired.

He nodded and we wound through a maze of wide, square columns and grid-aligned tables with people taking their afternoon coffee and tea. Toward the rear, a lesser-populated section appeared, and the hostess spoke again, "Here you are, Mr. Allen-Wilson. Just as yesterday, just as tomorrow, I suppose." She smiled at him, bowed slightly, turned and walked off.

The tall, lanky redhead pulled a seat from the table and nodded to me. As I sat, he pushed the chair in under me, as if he were my servant at home. He sat across from me, with Larion Dmitriyevich on my right, leaving one chair empty.

"Welcome to the Lily Pond, gentlemen," he intoned.

Stroop indicated the empty seat, "Are we waiting for another?"

"No. Not today, I'm afraid," his gaze dropped to the table.

"Lily Pond?" I asked.

Mr. Allen-Wilson nodded. "It is our 'special' section. A place where gentlemen of a certain persuasion can meet without fear of reprisal."

I peered around and realised that all the other customers were, indeed, men. Men with capes, men with canes, men with silk cravats. When I inhaled deeply, I noticed a new and different aroma, one that smelled a bit like oranges, but not as sweet.

"What is that scent?" I asked.

"Bergamot," Mr. Allen-Wilson answered. "The English are positively smitten with it." He closed his eyes and shook his head gently. "They have been putting in their tea for a hundred years, ever since Earl Grey began the silly tradition."

"It smells like a slightly-burnt orange," I observed, sniffing gently.

"It is, indeed, derived from the oil from the rind of a special citrus fruit grown in the south of France." His eyes darted about the room. "And since the perfumer Floris began adding it to their beloved Special Number 127, *everyone* has been wearing it." His hand swept across his body indicating the other patrons. "Simply everyone." He closed his eyes and shook his head again.

"Roy," Stroop spoke up. "Where is your Francis?" He pointed to the empty chair.

Mr. Allen-Wilson closed his eyes and took a breath before responding, "Francis got caught up in one of those raids last month. It's been over ten years since our beloved Oscar got sent to Reading Gaol, and almost six years since his early death." I could see a tear in one corner of his eye.

"A raid? Where was he?" Stroop asked.

"O, that I could tell you, Lary," his head drooped and shook from side-to-side. "A place that dare not speak its name. The shame of it all. He is now in Newgate awaiting sentencing."

Larion Dmitriyevich stood and walked behind his friend, who had begun to sob.

I had heard of Oscar Wilde's ordeal and his subsequent imprisonment. Stroop wanted to make sure I understood that the rest of the world was not as understanding as our native Russia when it came to the topic of men loving men. I did not think I could stand to live in a place where the very laws forbade my natural actions and choices.

Mr. Allen-Wilson put his hand in a coat pocket. "Oh! I nearly forgot. This telegram came for you just yesterday. I have no idea why, but it got sent to *my* home." He produced the sealed paper and handed it to Stroop, who quickly shoved it into one of his own pockets.

"Aren't you the least bit curious, Lary?" Mr. Allen-Wilson asked, eyebrows slightly raised.

Larion Dmitriyevich shook his head a few times. "Whatever it is, it can wait." He returned to his seat next to me. "Right now, I need to hear more about your Francis."

A server with a large, white apron approached and asked, "The same, Mr. Allen-Wilson?"

He nodded. "Earl Grey for three, please," and his face tilted downward

~ Π ~

For an hour or so, Stroop and Mr. Allen-Wilson spoke in hushed tones. The only phrases I could make out were: "Molly house," "London Bridge," "nightfall," "told him to use utmost caution," and "blasted, bloody Bobbies."

The Earl Grey tea tasted much like it smelled: subtle orange, but bland. Since we left Russia, I have found no beverage to replace our strong, smoky variety. If only they served Thibarine here.

While my companions went on with their whispered discussion, I glanced about at the fashionable menswear scattered throughout the "Lily Pond," as Mr. Allen-Wilson referred to this section of the coffeehouse. Most of the men wore stiff, high-collared white shirts beneath their tailored jackets. Pinstripes seemed most popular, but a few men had muted paisley patterns.

Many of the men also sported waxed moustaches, but few had beards. Stroop's blond goatee stood out, and not just because he happened to be the most handsome man in the room. I smiled at him, and he smiled back.

Outside on the pavement, Larion Dmitriyevich and Mr. Allen-Wilson shook hands vigorously. "And where are the two of you staying, Lary?"

"The Savoy on the Strand."

"Ah, I see. You like the modern touch."

"Well, as a matter of fact, yes, I guess I do at that."

"I wish I could have invited you to stay with me, but mother does not like visitors, you know."

"Oh, that is not a problem, Roy. We wouldn't want to put you out in any way. You already have enough on your plate, so to speak. We shall see you on the morrow."

We wouldn't want to put you out, Stroop said. He could have just as easily said, "I wouldn't want to put you out." It sounded like he had begun to think of me more than just an 'acquisi-tion' or a 'gentleman friend.'

Mr. Allen-Wilson stepped to the curb and raised his hand. A passing hansom stopped and he climbed in, having to duck his ginger head for fear of hitting it on the door frame.

"You seem to attract the redheads," I said in Russian so that no one nearby would catch it.

"What?" his face knotted quizzically. "Oh, Nata. Yes. The red-heads. Well, even with all his blubbering over his Francis, Roy is much more even-tempered than that blasted Kazansky girl back in St. Petersburg."

I wanted to add, "It wouldn't take much," but decided to keep that remark to myself as she was more than 1,500 kilometres away and no longer mattered.

Stroop began walking and I caught up with him. He stopped outside a building that looked somewhat like a brick firemen's hall. A sign above the wide, rectangular entrance read, "Piccadilly Circus Station."

"You are about to experience one of the wonders of the modern world. Wait here," he said before disappearing inside. I fol-lowed his movement as he went up to what appeared to be a banker's window. He returned with a small piece of paper with "3d" printed upon it. "Here, this is your ticket. Follow me."

Stroop and I went into the building and down a long set of stairs. The walls and arched ceiling were tiled, and I could de-tect the bouquet of stale urine. At the bottom, we stood on a platform within a circular, tiled tunnel. A few other people stood nearby, presumably waiting as well. Train tracks could be seen on the ground below, next to the platform. The wall opposite contained large adverts for beer, scotch, and cigars. I could see a tunnel at each end of the platform into which the tracks disappeared. Trains? Indoors?

A low rumble started followed by the rattling of metal parts. The platform beneath our feet began to tremble, and a shaky light approached from our left. Passenger cars without any visible locomotive stopped in the middle of the platform, and doors slid open. Stroop grabbed my hand and pulled me aboard. If he had not, I would have probably just stood gawk-ing at the luxurious coaches.

Instead of old, weather-worn wooden benches, the passenger car had a line of upholstered settees against the side walls facing each other. Well-dressed Londoners sat reading news-papers or books. Stroop sat and tugged me down next to him. Above our heads hung leather loops, and a handrail ran the length of each side.

The coach began to move, and we plunged into darkness, the only light came from electric lamps attached to the side walls.

"O, wonder!... O brave new world...," I recited, recalling Pros-pero's daughter Miranda from *The Tempest*.

"Did I not say that it was a wonder of the modern world?" Stroop reminded me.

"If only the trains in our mother Russia were so well-appointed I should never want to leave her again." I looked up and saw a broadsheet with a schematic of the rail lines. "And they all run through underground tunnels?"

"In the middle of London, yes, but as you move farther from the centre, the tracks go above-ground."

Our coach stopped, and the doors opened. On the wall behind the platform I could read, "Dover Street." Had they served meals, I would want to remain on this conveyance all the day. "How frequently does it stop?" I wondered how long it would be before we would have to disembark.

"Every few streets or so." The doors closed and the coach trav-elled once again.

"And how is it propelled? I saw no engine or locomotive."

"By electricity. No smoke, no steam." He smiled as if he had invented the system himself.

"Amazing!" *Such wonders, indeed*! It felt so futuristic.

"Down Street" proclaimed the next stop, and "Hyde Park" after that. When we reached "Knightsbridge," Stroop stood and walked to the platform. I really did not wish to follow him be-cause this had all been so new and exciting, but I realised without him I would probably starve, and the trains would most likely still be here later on.

The long stairway up felt like the price I had to pay for riding in such luxury. At the top, we exited the station and stood on Brompton Road. My head fell back as I looked up at the marvel of structures along the broad avenue, similar to Nevsky Prospekt in St. Petersburg.

"Come along, Vanya!" Stroop prompted. We walked a few blocks as I goggled and gawped at the line of stately buildings along the road. Autumn had arrived, and the trees lining the street had given up their leaves, which collected in ochre clumps along the curbs.

Soon we stood under a long awning that spanned an entire block. Large display windows tempted us to view the wares within. Mannequins modelled the latest fashions while posturing in a variety of staid poses. The word "Harrods" proudly shone in gold leaf from each pane.

"What is this place, Stroop?"

"A department store. The best in all of London, I dare say." He stepped to a wide set of ornate double doors, and a uniformed doorman pulled one open and held it for us. Inside I saw a bustling marketplace of goods. Rows and rows of glass-topped counters with salespeople in matching light green uniforms catered to yet more well-dressed Londoners.

"I feel like Moses on Mount Nebo, viewing the Promised Land but not allowed to enter," I looked up at Larion Dmitriyevich. "Why ever did you bring me here?"

"Come along, my *drozdik*. Heavenward we go," and he took my hand and led me to the base of a contraption I had never seen the likes of before. A wide swath of fabric running between two handrails rose from the floor at a gentle angle and ascended slowly to the next storey. The look of fear on my face must have prompted Stroop, "It's a moving staircase. You stand here at the bottom and it moves you up to the top without having to walk up the stairs."

I watched as others stepped onto the device and began to levitate upward. "Won't we be trapped at the top?"

He laughed at my naïveté. "No, silly. You step off the belt as you approach the next floor. Observe." Stroop pointed at the people who had just gotten on, and we watched them as they casually moved off at the top. "Come along." He grasped my sweaty hand again, and we both stood on the device. It shuddered and sputtered, but we slowly rose up and up. I could observe the layout of the entire ground floor filled with luxury items, perfumes and jewellery. Toward the rear of the store I could see men's wear. Near the end of the ride, Stroop said, "Watch this." With an exaggerated motion, he lifted one leg higher than it needed to be and placed it on the solid floor, followed by the other leg. I just jumped. It made more sense at the time because I did not want to get caught in the hungry-looking machinery. "Well, that works, too."

From there we walked back around to the base of the next moving sidewalk and went up yet again. The first floor had only lady's clothing. On the second floor, I saw soft goods and products for the home. Furniture on the third floor, and children's wear on the fourth. Once I had gotten used to the halting, jerky movements of the device, I began to really enjoy not having to walk up all those stairs. Perhaps they should have considered installing similar contraptions in the subway stations.

On the fifth floor, Larion Dmitriyevich secured salon services for the two of us. "Your hair has gotten a bit out of control, I believe. You look more like an Ancient Greek every day, but we no longer live in such times. You need to be modernised." I nodded, reflecting back to the last time I glanced in a mirror and saw what looked like a stork's nest perched upon my head. "I could use a bit of a shave myself..." He ran his finger along his smooth, beautiful neck.

A woman in a light green uniform guided each of us to separate chairs, and at the end of half an hour, I looked like a proper English lad. They had chopped off most of my hair, combed the rest directly back and oiled it with Macassar.

Stroop reappeared, looking even more dapper, and he smiled at my new hairstyle. "You look quite the thing, Vanya. Now we just have to get you a proper young man's suit. Come along."

Off we went, down the moving staircases this time. Would we stop on the fourth floor at children's wear or would he take me all the way down to the ground floor, to men's wear?

At the fourth floor, Stroop hesitated, looking in the direction of boys' wear. He looked back at me, shook his head and proceeded down the next moving staircase. Back down on the ground floor we worked our way through the grid of lustrous display cases to men's wear. I wouldn't have expected Larion Dmitriyevich to have an outfit tailored to fit me, and I did not mind when he went directly to the ready-to-wear section.

He pulled a few things off the rack and held them up, then put them back. A handsome man in a light green uniform appeared and asked if he could be of assistance. He and Stroop conversed while I made a circuit of the available suits. When I saw a grey suit with lilac pinstripes, I smiled, thinking back on "Uncle" Nika's suit. I pulled it off the rail and examined it. The cut looked smart but I was not sure of the size.

"Larion Dmitriyevich," I cried and his blond head turned my way. "Please look at this one." I held it up as he approached. A blank expression dominated his usually jocular face.

He then turned back to the shop assistant and waved his hand. The fellow stepped over. "Would this suit fit my... companion?" His other hand indicated me.

"Companion" sounded much better to me than "gentleman friend."

The assistant pulled a measuring tape from his coat pocket and began measuring my chest, my arm length, my waist, my inseam. He stood up and announced, "Your companion measures for a 32 Regular, and this particular specimen is a 36 Regular. Let me look in stock to see if we might have the item in his size." He turned and walked toward the rear of the store.

"Really, Vanya?" Larion Dmitriyevich questioned. "There are so many other jacket combinations. This is the suit you want?"

I nodded silently. There was no need to tell him the sad tale of my first train ride into St. Petersburg all those months ago.

The clerk returned with a paper-wrapped package. "Gentle-men, I happened to find this one what has not yet been opened. Would you like the young gentleman to try this on?" Stroop nodded. "Follow me, please." The clerk walked toward the rear of the store where the fitting rooms stood.

Once inside, I peeled off my Russian peasant garb and began to put on the pants.

"Here. You'll need this." A hand appeared through the curtain holding a white shirt. I took it and put it on.

When I looked at myself in the mirror, it appeared the jacket had been fashioned for me. The grey of the suit matched the grey of my eyes, and the lilac stripes could hardly be noticed. With my hair combed back, the arched eyebrows seemed even more prominent. I hoped I looked like a typical Londoner and that people would no longer think of me as the Travelling Prince, even though that misconception brought a few ad-vantages with it.

When I looked down at my bare feet, however, I realised there were a few more items of clothing I needed.

While a salesman fitted me for a proper Englishman's brown leather Oxford shoe, I watched Stroop take the telegram from his pocket and open it. He read it a few times, folded it up, and returned it to the pocket. His eyes drifted toward the ceiling, and the rest of his face relaxed. I hoped he would soon share with me what was in that message.

By the time we left Harrods, I had a new suit, shirt, socks, and shoes. It must have cost Stroop quite a bit of money, but I was sure I was worth it.

~ Π ~

Stroop insisted on taking a taxicab to the hotel because the nearest subway stop was too far away. I pouted for a bit, but when we pulled up to the hotel, my expression changed for the better.

The Savoy was a grand and stately building with a mansard roof and dormer windows. A sprawling awning covered the entrance, and the lobby looked so inviting, with tall, square columns and circular settees placed every so often.

Our room faced south, and through the large window I could see the Houses of Parliament and the Clock Tower across the Thames. London had proved to be ever so exciting. Stroop ordered a light meal for us to eat while we sat and watched the ships go by on the river. Afterward, he told me to get dressed because he had yet another surprise for me.

I did like surprises, especially when they were for me. As quickly as humanly possible, I donned my new suit and presented myself as ready. We left the hotel and walked across the plaza to the Savoy Theatre.

"Would you like to see how the English spend an evening?" he asked as if he didn't already know the obvious answer.

"Oh, yes, please!"

The performance that evening was Gilbert & Sullivan's *The Sorcerer*, a tale of love between a young man and his fiancée. Inside our box, the climate felt different. It took me a minute to figure out, but the ambient temperature seemed cooler than at other similar venues.

"Stroop?" I prompted, making him raise his head from the handbill. "The ambiance here is much more pleasant than at other theatres. Do you have any idea as to why?"

He nodded. "The lighting. It's entirely electric. No gaslights at all."

"Electricity! How marvellous! London is so modern!" I looked at the stage, the walls, the lights above. No flames or hurricanes. How very pleasant indeed.

In the operetta's tale, our young hero feared his fiancée would eventually weary of him, and he employed a travelling sorcerer to prepare a love philtre to assure their ever-lasting happiness. The favourable groom asked the magician to provide a sufficient quantity for the entire town so that everyone could enjoy the feeling of undying love; however, to prevent any impropriety, it would have no effect on married people. The unmarried townspeople gathered to partake of the philtre, and they all fell asleep as one.

From time-to-time during the performance, I looked out over the audience. Many of the people were reading from the libretto rather than watching the action on-stage. Every so often, I could hear the rustle of paper sacks and a crack! as someone bit into hard candy. The aroma of peppermint humbug wafted through the hall.

After the interval, when the people of the town awoke, each, in turn, fell madly, passionately in love with the first person they saw, which added quite a bit of comic effect because none ended up with their originally-intended partner. In the end the townspeople castigated the sorcerer, a colossal flame from the underworld consumed him, and the spell dissipated.

"And how did you enjoy the English opera, Vanya?" Stroop asked as we strolled back to our hotel room.

"Well, the tunes were catchier than most of the German and Italian works, most assuredly; however, the subject of love was handled with absurdity. Are the English not romantic?"

Larion Dmitriyevich threw his head back in laughter, which reverberated off the surrounding buildings on the plaza. "Vanya, this was a comic opera, like *Die Zauberflöte* or *Cosi fan Tutte.* The situations are contrived and manipulated for dramatic effect. Gilbert & Sullivan only wrote in this particular style. Their works are satirical and tongue-in-cheek."

"Oh, now I see. I particularly enjoyed how the entire chorus became part of the story. That is so rare in other operatic works."

"Yes, I guess that is so. How observant you are, my *drozdik.*" He smiled at me as we walked.

"Stroop, would you drink a love philtre with me to secure our never-ending love?"

His eyes peered back with intensity. "For one, I believe that no such thing exists, and, second, I believe that neither of us would require it, should one be available." He smiled and I smiled at him.

Upon entering the lobby, a gentleman at the desk called for Stroop, and he walked away as I stood waiting near the stairwell. He had still not shared with me the contents of the mysterious telegram. I wanted to ask him, and the thought began to consume me, but I knew him well enough not to press on this matter. I would have to trust that when the situation allowed, he would share his news with me, but that didn't make it any easier. After a minute, he returned and we walked up to our room together.

As it was rather late, we both removed our clothing and fell into bed. I tried to think about the likelihood of a real love philtre, but sleep quickly conquered me.

~ Π ~

In the morning, a dapper Mr. Allen-Wilson joined us in the Grill Room downstairs at the hotel. His expression appeared less distressed than yesterday.

"You're looking chipper this morning, Roy," Stroop stated as the two shook hands.

"Yes, well, I had a chance to visit my Francis, and it has made a world of difference. I now have some hope that I lacked previously." He smiled at me, "And you have had a change of outfit, young man."

I didn't know how to respond, and I just raised my eyes in Stroop's direction.

"I am glad to hear of your excellent tidings, Roy. It is good that you could meet us this morning as I have a big favour to ask of you."

"Today, Lary, I feel more prepared to deal with whatever you have to ask of me. What might that be, my friend?"

Stroop glanced at me and then at Mr. Allen-Wilson. "The cable you had received on my behalf was a request for me to appear at the Russian consulate for some reason. From here I must head to Chesham House in Belgravia." His face tightened, and I began to get nervous. He had not mentioned this to me.

"Nothing too terrible, I hope," the redhead quipped.

"I'm not sure. The only thing they sent was the invitation with no mention of the occasion." He smiled and glanced at me. "And that's where I need your assistance. Could you provide a tour of London for Vanya today?" A well-manicured hand landed on my shoulder.

"Why can't I gad about on my own?" I squeaked. "London seems much more tame than Alexandria."

"It most assuredly is safer, but Roy knows his way around, and you will use your time more wisely."

"Of course. And it will give us some time to get to know each other a bit better, yes?" Mr. Allen-Wilson smiled at me and I noticed a slight gap between his large front teeth.

I gritted my own teeth and smiled for their benefit. Someday I would be old enough to be on my own, but given the circumstances, I had to submit to Stroop's will.

We all stood, and I noticed Larion Dmitriyevich handing a few folded banknotes to his friend. He could have just given the money to me and let me pay for my food and incidentals. This arrangement, however, informed Mr. Allen-Wilson that I was unable to take care of my own self.

The three of us waited for a cab together without saying anything more. When one pulled up, Stroop told the driver where he needed to go, then turned to me. "I shall see you later for supper. Enjoy your day."

"Enjoy yours as well," I responded.

He climbed into the vehicle and it pulled away.

"Shall we?" asked Mr. Allen-Wilson indicating the sidewalk, and we began our tour.

"Where are we going?" I asked.

"I thought you might like to see the British Museum."

"Most definitely, but wouldn't that be kind of expensive?"

"Not at all! There is no charge to go in."

"No charge? How unusual. You English continue to amaze me."

"It's the best value in town!"

As we walked along Charing Cross Road, I said, "Stroop tells me you are descended from Scottish kings. Does that mean you are in line for the English throne?"

Mr. Allen-Wilson laughed nervously. "Well, while it is true that I can count King James of Scotland as an ancestor, that was quite a few generations ago. I believe that, at last count, I would be considered a ninth cousin to our King Edward."

"As well as our Tsar Nikolay Alexandrovich."

"True. They are first cousins, yes."

"But you are in line for the throne, no?"

"In a manner of speaking. However, at least a thousand people would have to die before they offered me the residence at Buckingham, I'm afraid." He smiled, and I smiled. This little bit of humour endeared me to him, and I decided not to make his hair colour an issue any longer.

"And what is it that you do, Mr. Allen-Wilson?"

"Do?" He looked down at me, head askew.

"As a means of earning money, I mean. Are you also in the same line of business as Larion Dmitriyevich."

His pink lips spread into a smile. "No. Not at all. I have no head for business, I'm afraid, young master." His gaze turned forward. "As it worked out, I sat Composition and have taken to writing."

"Are you an author, then?"

"Well," he hesitated, "of a sort. The type of things that I compose are... not for young people such as yourself. Perhaps, someday, when you are older, Lary will present you with a sample of my work."

"Yes. Someday. Perhaps." A most curious fellow. For a ginger person, I began to find him slightly attractive. I smiled up at him, and he smiled back.

We spent most of the rest of the day looking at antiquities in the British Museum. I wanted to spend more time looking at the Elgin Marbles than my tall companion could tolerate, and he walked off, leaving me on my own for a while. Seeing parts of the Parthenon and the Acropolis close up felt like a visit to Mount Olympus itself. The statues, metopes, and friezes depicted the denizens of classic mythology interacting, telling a story, or teaching a lesson.

I don't know how much time elapsed, but Mr. Allen-Wilson returned and said, "Vanya, I think it's time to move on."

At that moment, I happened to be viewing the bust of Antinous, considering the fate of the ancient lover to the Roman Emperor. I turned to my chaperone, "Is it far to visit Hadrian's Wall?"

He placed a thoughtful finger to his chin. "I believe, if I am not mistaken, that the ruins are over 100 kilometres north of here. It would be too far to travel in one day. Who is this strapping youth?" He pointed to the bust.

"Oh, this is Antinous, Emperor Hadrian's young male lover."

Mr. Allen-Wilson blanched, causing his freckles to stand out even more. He placed a loose fist to his mouth and coughed. "Hadrian's young male lover, you say?"

"Yes"–and now I had the opportunity explain something I had actually learned–"he was only nineteen when he died, presumably committing suicide by plunging into the Nile to save his master's life."

The redhead just stared at the marble. "And how old was the Emperor when this occurred?"

I had to do some maths in my head before arriving at an approximation. "In his early 50s, I believe."

"Ah, early 50s...," Mr. Allen-Wilson repeated, mostly to himself as if he were gazing into a mirror and speculating as to how old he appeared to others. While I had no idea of his actual age, I had to assume he was near to Stroop as they sat at university together, which would put him in his mid-30s; however, he appeared much younger, at least to me.

"Shall we?" he invited, and we strolled off to other exhibits.

By the end of our visit I had seen the Rosetta Stone, Cleopatra's sarcophagus, and a large carved stone head from Easter Island. I could have spent so much more time, but Mr. Allen-Wilson indicated we needed to return to the hotel in time to meet Stroop for supper.

"Can we take the underground trains, Mr. Allen-Wilson?"

He smiled, "The stations are not convenient. The amount of time we would spend walking to and from them would be just about the same."

I frowned because I had hoped to ride in the luxurious rail cars again. More than any other city I have experienced so far, London had captivated me in a way no other place had. It combined the sense of history that I enjoyed in Rome and Florence with a scientific modernity empowered by electricity. Walking about is quite pleasant, but there is also the underground train system. In addition, I got to use the English language and practise its eccentricities. Perhaps I could even attend an English school for boys if we were to stay for a while.

We arrived back at the Savoy Hotel just as Stroop returned.

"What chance!" Mr. Allen-Wilson quipped, but Larion Dmitriyevich glared at him. "Bad news, old chum?"

"If you like, you could join us at the River Restaurant," Stroop invited.

"That sounds wonderful! Thank you. I believe I shall."

Our table at the restaurant had the same spectacular view as our room, and I found it difficult not to look out the window at the twilight vista of majestic shadows across the golden Thames. I looked at Larion Dmitriyevich and he looked away. I had no idea as to what had upset him so.

He turned to Mr. Allen-Wilson. "Roy, I am glad you could join us because this shall be our final night in London."

"Final night?" I blurted out. "We just arrived."

Stroop turned to me, "Yes, I know, but the consulate has informed me that there are some… issues regarding my English citizenship, and we must leave."

"Oh, my," whimpered Mr. Allen-Wilson. "It was fortunate that we got to spend some time before you had to depart." He smiled at me. "And I truly enjoyed my day with your Vanya."

Not that I would have said it aloud, but I did enjoy my time with him as well. At first, I expected him to be much like the vituperative Nata, full of mercury and guile. However, as we discussed the enormous variety of displays at the British

Museum, I discovered Mr. Allen-Wilson to be well-educated and quite literate, possessing information regarding some of the items that were not recounted in their displays. It was like having my own private docent. He treated me with kindness and respect as well.

All-in-all, Mr. Allen-Wilson helped me to move past my prejudicial distaste for ginger-coloured people. I told myself to try not to judge others from their outward appearance.

Larion Dmitriyevich would not elaborate on the details of his meeting at the consulate, and for the rest of the evening he acted as if someone had tied a dead albatross about his neck. Even after returning to our room, we said very little to each other.

~ Π ~

After a light breakfast in our room, we headed back to the docks where we caught a small steamer to Helsinki. The previously-spectacular blue Thames turned to a murky greenish-brown, mirroring my sentiments about having to leave the city I had just fallen in love with. From Helsinki we boarded a ferry to St. Petersburg (perhaps even the same ill-fated craft I had taken that summer with the Kazanskys).

During the whole voyage back to St. Petersburg, Larion Dmitriyevich kept much to himself, hardly seeking my company at all. It worried me that upon our return he might set me free to find my own way once again. Now that I had some semblance of my own wings, I feared that my solo flight would resemble that of Icarus, and I would crash to the ground and my death.

Stroop secured a flat for us on the Vyborg Side close to where Stepan Stepanovich Zasadin, the Old Believer, lived. It was nowhere as grand as the apartment on Furshtadtskaya Street. He hired no house staff, and I slowly learned how to cook and make a home.

Once Larion Dmitriyevich began to emerge from his state of hibernation regarding the mysterious incident in London, we took regular afternoon strolls to the Summer Garden. He would meet me at my school and we would explore parts of the parkland we had not previous seen. He continued to educate me on the peculiar ways of the English language, and every so often, when necessary, Ancient Greek Grammar.

It was during one of our walks along the Swan Canal in the Summer Garden that I finally worked up the nerve to ask about our precipitous departure from London.

"I am truly sorry that I could not tell you at the time, Vanya, because it was so painful for me," Stroop said in English for fear that other people might overhear what he had to say. "It turned out that Scotland Yard–the Metropolitan London Police force–had observed my association with Roy, and that I was travelling with a young man to whom I had no familial ties. Back then, the new Lord Mayor, who had previously been Sheriff, was on a drive to enforce their laws regarding male couples. Roy was tied to his Francis, and you were connected to me. The Russian consulate made it clear that I had 24 hours to leave England or face imprisonment for my actions." He grimaced. "I never wanted you to learn of this because I feared you would blame yourself for bringing it about, and I knew how much you were growing to enjoy London. However, you asked." His eyes looked a bit puffy as he finished his explanation.

One corner of my mouth raised in appreciation of his valour, the other side remained flat because of the premature exodus from London. I stopped where we were, turned to Stroop, enveloped him with my arms, and kissed him full on the lips. "It doesn't matter where we are, my love"–I said in Russian, loud enough for anyone who might be passing by to hear–"as long as we are together." I grabbed his hand tightly in mine, and we continued our stroll as if nothing had transpired.

~ Π ~

With time we grew to be a loving and thoughtful couple, hosting those interminable social affairs that Stroop was so fond of. People making long-winded speeches glorifying ancient cultures whose bygone dust had settled into their venerable wrinkles.

As much as I wanted to keep a link with the city of London, I dared not ask Larion Dmitriyevich for the address of his school chum, Mr. Allen-Wilson, the tall, handsome, copper-headed fellow.

We spent evenings at the opera, and every so often we would run into one or another of the Kazanskys. Nata eventually found a pitiable suitable suitor who fell prey to her lack of charms.

I attended St. Petersburg State University to sit History and Ancient Studies. Once I graduated, I obtained a credential to instruct, and got hired on at the old school in Daniel Ivanovich's chair. Nikolayev and Shpilevsky had remained nearby, and both had taken chairs at the school as well. Our lunchtime discussions in the faculty room caused much impropriety and laughter, much to the dismay of the other, older teachers.

Writing poetry became my hobby, and Larion Dmitriyevich continued to deal in artefacts and relics sacred to the Old Believers. During my holiday time, we would travel to Greece and Italy together, reliving the days of our first encounters.

As Europe became tense and alliances collapsed and reformed, we hoped that calmer heads and peace would prevail. Unfortunately, during the summer of 1914, events in the Balkans led to a chain reaction of misunderstandings and posturing, leading to the formation of two great coalitions: The Central Powers and The Allies. Fortunately, Russia and England fell on the same side.

It was then that the Russian government decided that the Germanic-sounding "Saint Petersburg" should be replaced with the more Slavic "Petrograd." Of course, the inhabitants still referred to the city as "Petersburg." "Petrograd" only got used for official business and mail.

At first, the Russian military did not do well in their attempts to capture Prussia. A call went out for subscription, and Larion Dmitriyevich was required to report for duty.

"Must you fight, Larion Dmitriyevich?"

"I don't have much choice, my *drozdik*." He still called me that even though I now stood a few centimetres above him. "It is my duty, and I shall not shirk my responsibility, distasteful as it might be."

"Can't we flee to the south?"

He shook his head sadly. "All roads lead through Germany or Austria-Hungary."

"Ah." I had forgotten my geography. "And I suppose that England is out of the question." He nodded with a frown.

"I must report to the recruiter in the morning. I suggest we make the most of it while we can. Given the recent uncertain reports of our troops, there is no certainty as to how long these military actions should last. At best, I could return within a month."

"Stay, please, Larion Dmitriyevich, stay."

"Would that I could, my *drozdik*."

He clasped my hand, led me to our bed chamber, and we made our love as if it were the last time we would ever see each other again.

That evening, everyone we knew or cared about called upon us, and we had a flat full of merriment under a black powder cloud of impending warfare.

When Stroop reported for duty, I gave up the flat in St. Petersburg (or Petrograd, if you will) and returned to my little village in the middle-of-nothing with the hope of teaching the children in the farmlands about our glorious Greek and Roman predecessors.

Larion Dmitriyevich kept up a healthy correspondence, and he told me as much as he could without giving up military secrets. As I would have expected, he rose to officer status quickly, and he seemed to enjoy his exploits on the battlefields, all the while collecting spoils and souvenirs to bring home after the conflict ended.

With more time available to me, I began composing poetry again. Instead of attempting to recreate or imitate the works of other lands and cultures, I wanted to describe in words how it felt to be set adrift in a modern world with very few resources. In my poems, I attempted to capture the agony and exasperation of my early years and then contrast that with the happiness I had eventually found. After I completed each work, I read it aloud in my room, by myself, and then placed it in the desk drawer with the others.

In early 1916, the letters from Stroop halted abruptly. Because he had been unable to disclose his whereabouts, I had no idea where he might have been. At first, I tried to keep an optimistic head, hoping that he had been involved in campaigns in places where correspondence was not possible.

By May, my pessimistic heart had given up hope of ever seeing my beloved Stroop again, and it was no surprise when a face-less military officer showed up to convey the news of his death in battle. We had never travelled to the Nile together, but I would have willingly thrown myself into the roiling waters to save my man, much like Antinous did for his Emperor, Hadrian.

I wanted to cry over Stroop, but I think I had already used up my supply of grief during the foreshadowing months. The golden-orange sky of the plains turned a deathly-grey and my own eyes changed from steel to mud.

Days passed when I did nothing but sit in my little room and stare out the window at the gravid green fields across the way. I felt the land would soon lay fallow, as would I. None of my religious studies had prepared me for this eventuality. Not the Greek mythologies, not the various versions of Catholicism, not even Muhammadanism were able to assuage my deep heartache and anguish. The person who had provided me the life that I had always wanted was gone, and I would need to be my own man.

When I received news of a memorial service, I purchased a rail ticket and headed back to Petrograd.

Once again I found myself sitting on a splintered wooden bench (perhaps the same one as ten years ago) and watching groups of people in their various provincial costumes shuffle across the blistered red floor of an antiquated rail car and sitting on other benches. It was late May and muggy, even at this early hour. A liquefied sun disk peeked slowly over the hills to the east, cracking the murky sky. The shadowy outline of the city's squat apartment buildings appeared, and my mind flooded with memories, both welcome and unwelcome.

This is what prompted me to put my thoughts together and write them out so that others might discover, after we are both nothing more than bones in the desert, that for a few delightful years, two men learned how to live and love together despite their differences, despite the disproving beliefs of others, and despite the power of the gods to plant the seeds of disharmony. As I had learned from my experiences through mythology and opera, the gods could not themselves be happy if their earthly charges had larger and better wings than they did.

WAYNE GOODMAN has lived in the San Francisco Bay Area most of his life (with too many cats). When not writing, he enjoys playing Gilded Age parlor music on the piano, with an emphasis on women, gay, and Black composers.

Other Books by
Wayne Goodman

The Last Great Hope

A retired Secret Service agent, with a secret of his own, is called up for one last mission: find the long-lost child of John and Jacqueline Kennedy, whom he adopted out unknowingly under orders of his power-hungry boss.

Britain's Glory:
Charlotte, the People's Princess

Princess Charlotte was the daughter, and only child, of Princess Caroline of Brunswick and Prince George of Wales, eldest son of King George III. Destined to be Queen of Great Britain, her storybook life ended too soon, leading to a scramble for another, suitable, royal heir to take the throne.

The Seed of Immortality
Mahjong at Changshou Shan

Take thousands of years of Chinese culture, add three great philosophies, toss in a blue dragon with an agenda, arrange it all with Mahjong tiles, and you have "The Seed of Immortality." A peasant on his deathbed is given immortality by a less-than-trustworthy Mahjong sharp. They travel around China, learn its secrets, and even meet with the first Emperor of China in his mysterious subterranean palace, complete with rivers of mercury.

www.ingramcontent.com/pod-product-compliance
Lightning Source LLC
Chambersburg PA
CBHW070304120726
47910CB00007B/2365